Cameron's Crossing

Cameron's Crossing

Philip McCutchan

St. Martin's Press
New York

Library of Congress Cataloging-in-Publication Data

McCutchan, Philip.
    Cameron's crossing / Philip McCutchan.
        p.   cm.
    ISBN 0-312-09762-X :
    1. Cameron, Donald (Fictitious character)—Fiction.   2. Great Britain—History, Naval—20th century—Fiction.   3. World War, 1939-1945—Fiction.   I. Title.
    [PR6063.A167C338   1993]   93-24284
    823'.914—dc20   CIP

First published in Great Britain by George Weidenfeld and Nicolson Limited.

First U.S. Edition: October 1993
10 9 8 7 6 5 4 3 2 1

1

THE AIRCRAFT-CARRIER lay virtually helpless, at the mercy now not of Hitler's U-boats or of the long-range Focke-Wolfs and JU 88s but of the fiendish winter weather of the North Atlantic, the worst passage anyone aboard had ever experienced, even those officers of the Royal Naval Reserve who in peacetime had sailed aboard the liners of Cunard-White Star or Canadian Pacific. HMS *Charger* was one of the forty-odd escort carriers of around 15,000 tons provided by the United States under the Lease Lend agreement that had been of inestimable value to the British Navy, torn and depleted by the U-boat hunting packs in the early years of the war. Currently *Charger* was bound from Belfast to the US Naval Operating Base at Norfolk, Virginia, at the mouth of Chesapeake Bay. Under a reduced ship's company she was proceeding, not with a convoy, but independently and non-operationally with an escort of three destroyers, for long overdue refit and overhaul; and in her hangar she carried forty aircraft, outdated Avengers surplus to requirements, tightly packed in with folded wings and held fast to the deck by wire strops secured to ringbolts in the deck plating.

Or she had. Not now.

Well south of Iceland on her Great Circle track across the Atlantic she had met foul weather. The wind indicators on her navigating bridge had shown a wind speed of a little over 100 knots, with frequent gusts to around 120. The radar, at least until the antennae had been ripped away together with the main transmitting aerials, had shown echoes from mountainous seas, waves more than fifty feet in height. The welded seams down her sides had started to spring under the onslaught of the sea, with the result that the ingress of water was starting to flood down into the tiller flat where the steering engine was housed. If the steering went, *Charger* would be in immediate danger of broaching to, of being forced into the position of lying in the great troughs between the rearing waves, broadside to wind and sea. If that should happen her chances of coming through would be minimal.

The draft for the United States had entrained ten days earlier from the Royal Naval Barracks, Portsmouth, for Greenock on the Clyde. Their draft chits had indicated that they were to join HMS *Veracity*, one of the old V and W class destroyers, and that was all. The rating in charge of the draft, Chief Petty Officer Ben Malting, torpedo-coxswain, had made enquiries of the drafting master-at-arms in the barracks. He was old, at forty-nine, to be bucketing around U-boat-infested seas in a sieve, as he'd done ever since his recall from reserve and the comforts of running a pub in Queen Street hard by the barracks, back in '39. But he had been a small-ship man by his own choice on account of the compensations: a welcome absence of bull. No bugles and no brass hats, no falling in for Divisions and Evening Quarters like in the battleships and cruisers. You were a family in the small ships and you all suffered together, officers included. The wardrooms at sea were a pigsty just as much as were the messdecks. No crowd of stewards with white napkins, no gin and limes before a nicely served dinner, just bully beef and soaked clothing like the ratings.

'Know where she's lying, do you, eh?' Malting asked.

'Draft chit says the Clyde, don't it?'

'You know as well as I do,' Malting said, 'that don't necessarily mean much.' The Clyde in wartime had become a crossroads, ships and men coming in and going out again, going all across the world. A draft to the Clyde could mean anything really from Russian convoys to Trincomalee and the Far Eastern Fleet, or anything in between.

The master-at-arms wasn't giving anything away. Sealed lips were obvious. He said, 'How should I know? I'm not Winston Churchill. And if I did know, I wouldn't be saying.' He aimed his pencil at Malting. 'Remember the posters, eh? Be Like Dad, Keep Mum.' He gave a sudden guffaw of laughter. 'That other one an' all . . . 'Itler and Goering sitting in a bus an' two old biddies right ahead of 'em . . . one old biddy saying to the other you never know who's listening. Tickles me sense o' humour does that one.'

It was mid February. When the draft for the *Veracity* detrained at Upper Greenock station, to be met by naval transport into which they piled their kit-bags and hammocks, it was bitterly cold and snowing hard. When the transport turned them out at Albert Harbour they could barely see across the Tail o' the Bank towards Helensburgh on the farther shore. Through the snow many shapes loomed like sea-borne ghosts, battleships and battle-cruisers – Malting recognized *Nelson* and *Renown* – aircraft-carriers of various sizes, cruisers, destroyers . . . the main weight of the navy had shifted north to the Clyde and the Firth of Forth once war had broken out, leaving the great peacetime bases of Portsmouth and Devonport and Chatham more or less deserted. There were many merchant ships as well – probably, Malting thought, a convoy forming up. One giant two-funnel job was immediately recognizable as the liner *Queen Elizabeth* and never mind the wartime grey camouflage paint appropriate to her role as a troop transport.

'Typical bloody Clyde,' a voice said alongside Malting. Petty Officer Berridge, chief bosun's mate to be of the *Veracity*, a Royal Fleet Reservist like Ben Malting, was a moaner; a decent enough bloke and always on the top line at his job, but a moaner. He and Malting had been shipmates before, China-side and the Mediterranean Fleet in

3

peacetime, and they were good friends mostly. Having taken his pension back in 1936, Berridge had been a regular at Malting's pub – very regular, in order to escape the wife and have a good moan about her. Mrs Berridge had once, just once, come in with him; and Ben Malting, who hadn't met her before, had summed her up as a walking vinegar bottle. She'd sat bolt upright on a chair, her handbag clasped in both hands and held rigidly on her knees while her beady eyes had moved from side to side looking at likely women – Ben had always been a skirt chaser – especially at Ben's barmaid Dolly Fewkes who happened to be very well endowed titwise. PO Berridge, however, had watched his step that night and his visits had been just as regular thereafter.

'Clyde's all right in good weather, Archie.'

Berridge grunted. 'You know what they say. If you can see across the Clyde it's going to rain. If you can't, it's raining already. That's when it's not snowing.' He brought out a handkerchief and sneezed hugely. 'See? Got to me tubes right away. What do we do now, eh? Get bloody soaked right through our bleedin' oilskins?'

Malting said, 'Keep the lads fallen in, Archie, and I'll report to Navy House.'

Navy House was a requisitioned office building at the back of the small basin that formed Albert Harbour, which was filled with picquet-boats from the fleet and with drifters that acted as tenders to the ships, ferrying libertymen and so on. As CPO Malting made his way along the greasy stones of the dockside, an officer hunched into a bridge coat bearing on the shoulders the wavy gold stripes of a lieutenant-commander of the Royal Naval Volunteer Reserve came out and approached the draft. Malting saluted.

'Party on draft for *Veracity*, sir.' That was when he recognized the officer, last seen as a two-striper in white tropical rig in West Africa, not then, as now, muffled to the eyebrows. 'Well, Lord bless my soul, sir, if it's not Mr Cameron!' He took in the half stripe. 'Beg pardon, sir. Lieutenant-Commander Cameron.'

'It's me all right, chief, and glad to see you.' Cameron reached out a hand: they shook warmly. 'I asked for you as cox'n and the drafting people let me have you.' He grinned. 'If they hadn't, I'd have raised hell and they knew it.'

'You taking over the *Veracity*, are you, sir?'

Cameron nodded.

Malting said, 'Then she'll be a happy ship and a good one, sir.'

'I hope so – with your assistance, Cox'n.' Coxswains of destroyers and the smaller ships were the senior lower-deck ratings aboard and were to their captains and first lieutenants what a regimental sergeant-major was to the colonel and the adjutant. Ramrods and advisers, the men who stood between the wardroom and the messdecks and had a finger on the pulses of both, the mainstay of the ship, reliable and immensely loyal to a good co, hand-picked for their rate. And Cameron knew that Malting was one of the best; Malting felt the same way about Cameron, whom he had met and come to admire a couple of years previously on the West African coast.

Cameron asked, 'How's Mrs Malting?'

'Chokker, sir. Me being drafted out of barracks. You know what women are like. She'll get used to it like she always has. And the pub, it'll keep her occupied.'

Cameron nodded. 'Telephone home, Cox'n. There's a public box in Navy House. Let her know you've got here.'

'Well – thank you very much, sir – '

'In the meantime I'll have a word with the lads.' Cameron paused. 'Who's the buffer to be?'

'PO Berridge, sir. Old mate o' mine. He's a good bloke. We get along together.'

'That's a good start,' Cameron said. Malting went off through the snow to make his telephone call. Just like Mr Cameron to think of that, even remember he had a wife and a pub. Malting still had no idea where the *Veracity* was currently operating but of course he wouldn't have said anything to Bessie even if he had, and Mr Cameron would

5

know that. In wartime, you watched your tongue. The perishing Nazis had ears all over the show.

The drifter was seen nosing in through the harbour entry, nudging the bluff of the wall with her fenders, pushing through the falling snow towards where the draft ex-Pompey Barracks was fallen in, 134 ratings of the various branches, deck, signal staff, engine-room, cooks and stewards and so on, seeking what shelter they could find from the wind-blown snow that found its way beneath oilskins and down collars, turning the piled kit-bags and hammocks into a white-covered mound. Cameron had been joined by four more officers, two lieutenants of the Royal Naval Reserve, the professional reserve found from officers of the merchant fleets, the liners and tankers and dry-cargo ships; and two officers wearing the single thin straight stripe of a warrant officer RN. One of these also wore a thin purple stripe: the warrant engineer evidently. The other, Malting assumed, would be either a gunner or a gunner (T). He hoped it wouldn't be the latter: a gunner (T), a WO of his own branch, might prove a pain in the arse for all he knew; whereas a plain gunner, product of Whale Island or the Chatham or Devonport gunnery schools, didn't know too much about the torpedo department even if he thought he did and when necessary could be submerged in the bullshit that according to naval regulations always baffled brains. As the drifter came alongside its skipper leaned from the wheel-house and called across.

'Party for the *Charger*?'

Malting was about to answer no when to his surprise Cameron said, 'That's us.' He turned to Malting. 'Get them aboard, please, Cox'n. Have a party ready to take the bags and hammocks.'

'Aye, aye, sir.' Malting saluted and carried out the order. This was just what he'd hinted to the drafting jaunty back in RNB. The perishing *Veracity* wasn't anywhere near the Clyde and they were due to take passage to God alone knew where and even He wouldn't say. Except via the earthly form of

6

Lieutenant-Commander Cameron in due course. Cameron had always been a good bloke at keeping the hands informed whenever it was possible for him to do so.

With the bags and hammocks embarked and the draft aboard, the drifter moved out for the anchorage at the Tail o' the Bank, threading through the lines of snow-covered ships waiting for the orders that would send them out again to sea. As for a brief while the snow lessened, the farther shore of the Clyde became visible, showing the buildings of Helensburgh and the great hills rearing over the Gair Loch, the Holy Loch and more distantly Loch Lomond. The hills were white now and impressive enough but to the jaundiced eyes of the naval draft wondering about their destination they had little hint of romance or of high roads and low roads . . . today the banks of Clyde were very far from bonny, very ill suited to any roaming in the gloaming . . . and the sun had no need to go to rest. It hadn't been visible all day.

'You down there.'

Cameron looked up as the loud voice cut through the murk. The drifter was approaching the escort carrier's starboard for'ard sponson down from which led the accommodation ladder. A lieutenant RNVR stood there with his gangway staff of quartermaster and bosun's mate; but the voice had come, like that of God, from on high – from the navigating bridge, over the guardrail of which could be seen a very red face beneath a cap whose brim carried a row of gold oak leaves. On the shoulders of the bridge coat were the four straight stripes of a captain RN.

Cameron called back, 'Yes, sir?'

'Are you in charge?'

'Yes, sir – '

'Then kindly don't delay.' There was an autocratic snap in the voice: Captain Mason-Goodson was not a man who liked to be kept waiting. 'That damned drifter should have been alongside fifteen minutes ago and now I'm up against my sailing time. Those damn drifter skippers are all the same.'

Cameron was about to make some kind of polite response when the window of the drifter's wheelhouse went down at the rush and a stream of what was undoubtedly invective came out. The drifters that serviced the Tail o' the Bank had been conscripted down from the fishing grounds in the far north-west of Scotland and the tongue was difficult to follow: but the gist was that the skipper had scant time for the Royal Navy. Captain Mason-Goodson called down again.

'What was all that?'

The skipper made an effort, became more intelligible. 'Get stuffed,' he shouted.

'What damned impertinence! I shall make a report to the Flag Officer in Charge.'

A fist was waved from the wheelhouse window. 'Report to whom ye bluidy wish and much good may it dae ye. I own ma bluidy boat. Ye dinna own yours.' The window was pulled up again. The brass hat vanished from the bridge. Cameron suspected much high dudgeon. He grinned as he caught Malting's eye. Malting responded with a wink. He was glad his rate as torpedo-coxswain protected him from aircraft-carriers, and never mind the discomforts that awaited them all aboard the *Veracity*. Wherever she might be.

The embarkation was smartly carried out under the eyes of Malting and Berridge after Cameron and the other officers had climbed the ladder to the sponson to be saluted aboard. Cameron was informed that the Captain wished to see him on the bridge as soon as the ship had cleared through the boom running across from Dunoon to the opposite shore.

He suspected a bollocking.

2

As the carrier's anchor, the cable already shortened in, was brought home to be held on the brake to lie at the waterline until the ship had cleared close waters, the engine-room telegraph was moved to slow ahead. Cameron, as he followed the bosun's mate below to the cabin allocated to him, felt the pulse of the engine as the single screw began turning. Unaccustomed to big ships, he felt a sense of disorientation: the carrier seemed to be all echoing spaces, the hangar through which he had been taken more like a vast barn than anything he would have connected with a ship; after that, a number of steel ladders leading down into shining steel alleyways off which the officers' cabins opened. These cabins were shielded from the alleyways by curtains only, no doors; and mostly they were two-berth affairs. Cameron remembered that the *Charger* was American-built to American standards. He was relieved to find that as a lieutenant-commander he had been allocated a single-berth cabin. Aboard a ship your cabin was the only place where you could expect privacy, and Cameron valued his privacy when he could get it.

When his gear had been brought down by a party of seamen, Cameron went on deck, making a start on familiarizing himself with the ship's layout. From the walkway running alongside the immense flight deck with its barrier and tripwires, he looked out at the familiarity of the Clyde. He'd

9

sailed from there often enough, had made many a return there too, glad after many months away at sea to be, once again, sailing up the Clyde from Ailsa Craig, past the great peaks of Arran and the flat lands behind Ayr and Ardrossan on the opposite shore, on through the Cumbraes, past Rothesay Bay and Largs and Dunoon for the Tail o' the Bank and a Scottish homecoming. Now, once again, it was the other way round.

Already the carrier was turning to port in her approach to the anti-submarine boom. Cameron left the walkway and entered the bridge superstructure. Better not to keep the Captain waiting again. . . .

Berridge was having a moan about the accommodation allocated to the chief and petty officers. 'Perishin' bunks,' he said in disgust. 'Beds is all right ashore, but I don't reckon I can sleep in a bloody bed at sea.' Hammocks were more stable; the ship rolled round them, they themselves remained steady unless you were cack-handed enough to sling them athwartships instead of fore-and-aft. 'I s'pose the Yanks like them or they wouldn't have 'em, eh?'

Malting said, 'You'll be back in a mick soon enough, Archie.'

'Roll on the day, mate! Norfolk, Virginia – might have guessed it.' They had already picked up the buzz, the ship's destination. '*Veracity*'s been in for action damage, I reckon.'

'We'll be finding that out. Skipper'll not keep us in the dark long.'

'You reckon?' Berridge sat down on his bunk. He was a tall man and big. The back of his head struck the metal frame of the bunk above and he swore. 'Talk about claustrophobia. You'd think they'd have more room in an aircraft-carrier, eh?' Then he brightened. 'States, eh? Should be compensations, Ben. All those popsies in uniform. Waves, they call 'em. Or something like that. Make – '

'You're too old for that lark, Archie. They'll call you grandad.'

There was no talk of war, of dangers lurking in the North Atlantic. To men accustomed to small ships, there was a strange remoteness about an aircraft-carrier, as though she was too fat a duck ever to be involved in real war.

On the bridge Cameron saluted Captain Mason-Goodson, whose four stripes were now hidden beneath an immense buff-coloured duffel-coat against the worsening weather. 'You wished to see me, sir.'

There was a grunt. 'And you are?'

'Cameron, sir, taking passage. Commissioning *Veracity* in Norfolk.'

'Ah, yes. That drifter. I've made a report. FOIC'll have that feller's balls for breakfast.'

'I'm sorry, sir – '

'Not your fault.' So there wasn't to be a bollocking. Mason-Goodson stared thoughtfully at the stripes on Cameron's bridge coat shoulder-straps. 'RNVR,' he said, as though an RNVR officer taking up a command was somehow not quite the thing. 'I suppose you'll cope.'

'I believe I will, sir. *Veracity* won't be my first command.'

'There's no need to sound argumentative, Cameron.'

Cameron gaped, but thought better of a tart reply. He said, 'I'm sorry, sir.'

Mason-Goodson lifted his binoculars and stared ahead through the driving snow. Largs Bay was coming up on the port bow, Toward Point to starboard at the entrance to Rothesay Bay. Further ahead lay the Cumbraes, after passing which the carrier would stand clear in the wider waters of the Firth. The Captain spoke again. 'I trust you'll keep your ship's company active – on their toes.'

'Yes, sir.'

'Nothing worse for morale than having too little to do. See that they get to know my ship in case we meet trouble. Liaise with my executive officer.'

'Yes, sir.' Cameron hesitated. 'My officers and I . . . we'd like to take a share of the bridge watchkeeping, sir, if you – '

'If you're required, Cameron, you'll be told soon enough. But with only small-ship experience I doubt if you'd be much use on the bridge of an aircraft-carrier.' Mason-Goodson lowered his binoculars. 'It might be useful if you took a watch with one of my officers. As understudy.'

When one of the carrier's destroyer escort had started signalling with her Aldis lamp, Cameron had been summarily dismissed from the Captain's presence. He went below seething: he wasn't prepared to act as anybody's understudy and said so to his first lieutenant, Neil Grey, an RNR who in peacetime had been second officer of a cargo ship trading to the Far East.

'What if you're given the order?' Grey asked.

'I'll plagiarize that drifter skipper,' Cameron answered with a short laugh.

'And face Court Martial. It's not worth it.'

'Well, I'll cross that bridge when I reach it, Number One. In the meantime you and I had better get together on working out a programme of exercises for the ship's company. I'd like to formulate our own ideas ready to face the ship's executive officer with them. Have you encountered him, by the way – the Commander?'

Grey nodded. 'A brief word – he seems a decent enough sort. RN and a shade formal, but otherwise human. Bought me a gin in the wardroom,' he added. 'Didn't have one himself, had to leave when Special Sea Dutymen were piped. I thought it was a kindly gesture of welcome aboard, so there's hope yet!'

Cameron grinned. 'Something tells me you don't like the big-ship life any more than I do!'

'You're dead right. Too many odd bods floating about with not enough to do. I suppose it'd be worse if there was a Fleet Air Arm squadron embarked.'

Cameron agreed; but the fact of the ship being non-operational did in fact leave a somewhat naked feeling. An aircraft-carrier deprived of her teeth, her fight-back, was a very large and vulnerable target despite the destroyer escort. And, just as Petty Officer Berridge had noted, Cameron felt claustrophobic down below in the carrier's sheer immensity. Apprehensive, too: so many ladders to climb to the upper deck . . . and down below the plating of the escort carriers was paper-thin. In his cabin as the ship moved out from the Cumbraes Cameron had been able to hear the surge and hiss of water a matter of centimetres from his bunk. That was the measure of safety, the measure of all that stood between the ship's company and the inrush of water if a torpedo or a shell should hit.

By next morning, with the carrier clear of the Bloody Foreland at the north-west tip of Ireland and heading behind her escort into the Atlantic on her Great Circle track for the United States, Mr Trimby, warrant engineer, had made his number with the ship's chief engineer, an RNR named Chatterton, a lieutenant-commander(E) who in peacetime had been chief aboard a Cunarder. Mr Trimby had been taken on a tour of the engine spaces, a matter of professional interest. But Trimby's attention wandered; he had other things on his mind and they were to do with his domestic affairs. His appointment to the *Veracity* couldn't have come at a worse time: his marriage was in danger of breaking up, to put it mildly: he'd been caught in a compromising situation with his wife's sister in the front room of his house in Wolverhampton. The wife's sister had been much keener on it than Maud herself and the actual situation had been much too compromising for any explanation to have a snowflake in hell's chance of success. Maud had flown into a tearing rage and had attacked her sister, and himself, with flung china, including a much loved teapot that had been Mr Trimby's mother's. There had been a good deal of wreckage and then Maud had rushed to the kitchen and come back with a carving knife. The sister had fled into the street yelling blue murder and had run into the arms of a policeman pounding his beat. The bobby had sensibly put it down to a domestic tiff, had persuaded them all to sit down over a nice cup of tea, in which he had partaken himself, had given them a talking-to, and had departed. So that was all right; no charges about disturbing the peace or attempted murder. But it had been unpleasant for Mr Trimby, and undignified for anyone wearing (more or less anyway) the uniform of a warrant officer in His Majesty's Navy, to be propelled indoors by the arm of the law and spoken to like a naughty child. And, of course, that had not been the end of it in Maud's view. There had been another scene and floods of tears and recriminations and Maud had flung out of the house to be followed by her equally tearful sister in a state of remorse. Mr Trimby had finished his embarkation leave on his tod, cooking and all, and hadn't set eyes on his wife, or her sister, since. A letter had been delivered by the postman three days later, just catching him before he left for the railway station under orders for the Clyde, indicating that Maud was consulting a solicitor. She had not given her current address.

Mr Trimby, reflecting on all this as the carrier's chief engineer waffled on, found his thoughts interrupted by the strident racket of the alarm rattlers.

The sea's surface was a flat calm, disturbed only by the beginnings of an ocean swell. The snow was still falling, and the watchkeepers on the bridge found the flakes settling deeply on their duffel-coats, the hoods of which were pulled over their uniform caps. It would have been hard in the snow-reduced visibility for the lookouts, sweeping all around with their binoculars, to pick up the feather of water that would indicate the presence of a submarine at periscope depth; but the contact had been reported by the Asdics and the senior officer of the destroyer escort had passed the warning by Aldis lamp.

The yeoman of signals reported to the Officer of the Watch. 'From *Invergarry*, sir, contact bearing red four five, distant eight cables.'

The Captain had gone below a few minutes earlier. The

word was passed to his cabin; he was back on the bridge within thirty seconds. As he came up the ladder at the rush action stations was sounded and almost simultaneously the sound of exploding depth charges reached the ship: the escort had been right on the ball. Below in the engine-room, Mr Trimby felt the percussion. Everything seemed to shake. Cameron, sitting in the wardroom with Neil Grey, went fast up the ladders to the hangar, and out onto the port for'ard sponson where he met the snow and the keen wintry air. He and Grey were joined by Chief PO Malting.

'See anything, sir?' Malting asked.

'Too much snow,' Cameron answered. He turned to Grey. 'I'm going to the bridge, Number One.' Shortly after leaving the Clyde the ship's commander had allocated action stations to the ratings taking passage: the seamen were to stand by the guns as replacements if required, the engine-room artificers and stokers were to stand by the air-lock into the engine-room, the cooks and stewards and other miscellaneous categories were to muster at the fore end of the hangar and await orders. The officers had been allocated no precise stations but were to be generally handy, taking any orders from the Captain or Commander.

As Cameron reached the bridge the depth-charge attack seemed to come nearer, not far now to port. The heavy thuds rang through the ship's thin plates, shook the bridge itself. Then, very suddenly as the great spouts of disturbed water thrust upwards, something else was seen, dimly through the falling snow: a long black shape emerging drunkenly from the sea, rolling badly and down by the head, water streaming from the washports in her conning tower and off the pressure hull.

All the binoculars trained upon the U-boat. 'Damaged,' Captain Mason-Goodson said briefly. 'She's not going to last, that's obvious.'

'Survivors, sir?' the navigating officer asked.

'Leave the buggers, pilot. I'm not risking my ship – there may be other U-boats in – ' He broke off as aboard the U-boat men were seen to be swinging the machine-gun round to bear on the carrier, and other men emerged from a hatch in the fore plating and ran to the casing-mounted three-pounder. 'Wheel hard-a-starboard, pilot, engines to emergency full ahead!'

'Aye, aye, sir.' The orders were passed to the wheelhouse; the telegraph rang, an urgent sound as the handles were pulled over twice in indication of emergency, then the orders were repeated from the starting platform below. Before the bulky carrier had begun her swing away, the German guns had opened. Machine-gun bullets swept the port sponsons and the walkways just below the flight deck, swept the open quarterdeck below the round-down of the flight deck's overhang. Then the three-pounder opened, scoring a hit on the port side of the hangar. There was no explosion. A few moments later a report came from the hangar: the projectile had penetrated the ship's side without exploding and was currently being extricated by a party of seamen under the chief gunner's mate. It would be jettisoned overboard from the nearest sponson.

'Sooner them than me,' Mason-Goodson said. 'Pilot?'

'Yes, sir?'

'I'm maintaining full starboard wheel until we've turned through three-sixty degrees. Then I'll steady her. My intention is to finish the enemy off by ramming.'

'Assuming the bow plating will take the strain, sir.'

Mason-Goodson swung round, staring. 'Are you arguing with me, pilot?'

The navigator stood his ground. 'Not arguing, sir. Just pointing out the possibilities.'

'Which comes to the same thing. I have given an order, navigator. You will obey it.'

The navigator shrugged. The Captain repeated, 'My intention is to ram. Warn the engine-room. And pass by Tannoy, all hands throughout the ship to be ready for an impact for'ard. Where's that RNVR, Cameron, isn't it?'

'Here, sir,' Cameron said, and the Captain swung round onto him.

'You can make yourself useful, Cameron, earn your keep. Nothing's been heard from aft since the German opened. Go along, see what the state is, and take charge.'

'Aye, aye, sir.' Cameron saluted and turned to leave the bridge. The swing continued under full wheel; the carrier's decks were tilted at a difficult angle for the descent of the many ladders and it was hard to maintain a foothold on the greasy deck of the hangar, where the embarked aircraft were straining at the wire retaining strops. Men were still working on the unexploded projectile from the U-boat, and Cameron could see the hole in the side and the jags of metal around it. As he moved aft, a big explosion came from the quarterdeck. He carried on as fast as he could, past the after aircraft lift-well and thence out onto the open quarterdeck where the twin 4-inch, the carrier's main gun armament, was situated.

Or had been.

The guns were still there, but had been half torn from their mounting, one barrel twisted into a knot. The ready-use ammunition locker had been shattered and the after end of the hangar was pock-marked as though hit by flying metal fragments. There was blood everywhere, and bodies. Cameron looked in horror at the carnage, found no living soul; the whole gun's crew had been taken out, no doubt by the machine-gun fire as well as impact of the three-pounder shell and the exploding ammunition. One of the seaman gunners lay half across the guardrail, blood still pouring from his neck; the head was hanging by a thread as it seemed, and as Cameron watched, sick to the guts, it fell away into the sea. There was a curious silence now, a silence of death broken only by the swish of the sea past the carrier's hull, no more firing from the German guns. The snow went on falling, the flakes settling on the broken bodies, on a leg that had somehow got itself wrapped around the twists of the gun barrel. The settling snow reddened. It was a scene from very hell.

There was nothing Cameron could do. He stumbled back

into the hangar. He met the Commander coming aft, and he reported.

'Medics,' Commander Warren said.

'Too late, sir.'

'All the same. . . .' The Commander turned to his seaman messenger and sent him to inform the surgeon lieutenant-commander. Cameron climbed back to the bridge. Captain Mason-Goodson was wedged into a for'ard corner of the bridge and was staring intently ahead, his body hefted over the glass screen so that he could get a clearer view through the snow. He looked over his shoulder as Cameron stood behind him. 'Well?' he asked.

Cameron reported again.

'Too bad,' Mason-Goodson said. That was all; his attention returned to the U-boat, which was still wallowing and now that the carrier had completed her turn lay dead ahead, inertly waiting for the impact of some 15,000 tons of metal moving at maximum speed. There was still no more firing. As Cameron watched, men were seen to be jumping from the U-boat's casing into the sea, deserting the guns, knowing now what was in the carrier Captain's mind. They would probably be expecting to be picked up later.

Captain Mason-Goodson stood like a statue as the carrier moved on, the wind made by her passage whipping the snow into the faces of the men on the bridge till the flakes stung like icicles. As the target began to vanish below the fore end of the flight deck, Mason-Goodson spoke again.

'Now,' he said. 'Hold tight, all of you.'

Then the impact came. There was the scream of tortured metal as the racing bows bit into the U-boat's pressure hull. Cameron, holding onto a stanchion, felt as though his arms were being torn from their sockets. The yeoman of signals crashed past him, went flat on the deck, his head impacting on the fore screen. The navigating officer sprawled over the binnacle, legs and arms waving like some immense duffel-coated spider, all the wind knocked from his lungs. As the ship continued ahead at reduced speed, the U-boat was seen to have been cut neatly in two, her fore part banging its way down the carrier's starboard side, her after end doing likewise to port. The men who had gone overboard were still to be seen in the water, some of them waving their arms, some of them shouting.

Mason-Goodson left them to it. He gave his orders. 'Resume your course, pilot. Shipwright's party to sound round for'ard. Report the condition of the collision bulkhead – engine to slow ahead until the shipwright's reported to me. Inform my steward I'll now have a delayed breakfast here on the bridge. Yeoman?'

'Sir?' The yeoman of signals was still breathless but was on his feet again, undamaged apart from a lump on his head and a neck that felt half-way broken.

'Make to *Invergarry*, I have resumed course and will steam at slow speed until any damage has been assessed.' Mason-Goodson paused. 'Add, I consider your Asdics should have picked up the enemy before he became a close danger to my ship. I propose informing Admiralty of my displeasure on arrival in USA. That's all, yeoman.'

There was no vital structural damage, just a large dent in the bow plating and a small fracture that was admitting a little water. A temporary running repair would be made easily enough and shortly the ship would be able to resume normal speed. The collision bulkhead was intact. The doctors were being kept busy with injuries resulting from the impact – bruised flesh, some broken limbs, and Warrant Engineer Trimby suffering from a good deal of tenderness in a part of his body that, had the incident occurred before his last leave, would very likely have saved his marriage: remaining below with the ship's engineer officer, his grip on a solid object had not withstood the impact of ramming and he had been thrown from the starting platform to fetch up with a handwheel on a valve lodged painfully between his legs. Moaning in agony he had wondered whether this could have been the hand of

God. . . . The swelling was unlikely to go down for quite a while, he was told later by the PMO.

Cameron was frank with his first lieutenant, strictly in private and strictly between the two of them. 'Mason-Goodson's a cold fish. Breakfast – with all those Jerries in the drink, just left to drown.'

'The exigencies of war. It's been done often enough before, sir.'

'Yes, I know, but . . . well, there was absolutely no remorse, no sign of regret over what I agree might have been an inevitable decision. Also – another point and a worse one –he seemed quite unconcerned about what happened to his own gun's crew. I reckon he was responsible for their deaths, Number One. If he hadn't turned his stern slap towards the U-boat, given the buggers a good target they couldn't miss, it wouldn't have happened. Oh, I know all the arguments, you have to accept risks and all that . . . the point is, he just didn't seem to care.'

'It's not our worry,' Neil Grey said. 'We're just taking passage, that's all. Once we're over the other side, we can forget about Mason-Goodson.'

Not so easily, Cameron thought. He believed that the cold-fish attitude of Mason-Goodson was not going to be lost on his ship's company. He didn't seem the sort of captain that men would follow as it were to the death. He was too emotionless, too self-centred, Cameron believed. They still had all the North Atlantic to cross. He hoped there wouldn't be any more contact with the enemy while he, Cameron, and his own men were in the hands of Captain Mason-Goodson although in general, he had to admit, he was unable to fault the Captain's conduct of the action. It had been a successful action resulting in the destruction of a U-boat. At the same time the doubts remained.

The passage-takers were kept active. When the aircraft-carrier had left the snow behind and was steaming in fair weather, the ship's physical training instructor, a petty officer, fell in all hands of leading rate and below for PT on the flight deck. Cameron and Grey attended as spectators, freezing in the cold air until Cameron suggested they join in themselves. They did so; but when the first session was over, Cameron was sent for to the bridge, where Captain Mason-Goodson was looking sour, the red face frowning blackly.

'Damned undignified, Cameron. Don't do it again.'

'Sir?'

'You know very well what I mean. Putting yourself on the same level, don't you know. The men don't respect officers who play to the gallery.'

Cameron was furious. 'I'm sorry, sir. Aboard my own ship I've always – '

'Kindly don't argue with me, Cameron. You're not aboard your own ship, you're aboard mine. And I won't have it.'

'Sir, I – '

'That's all, Cameron.' Mason-Goodson turned his back. Cameron went down the ladder, seething. Mason-Goodson had it all wrong; there had been no attempt to play to the gallery, merely to take part in an exercise period that was always unpopular with seamen who wished only, when off watch at sea, to climb into their hammocks for a zizz, or play tombola in the messdecks, or write a letter home, or just sit and daydream till the bosun's calls piped them to something more active. However, there it was; *Charger* was Mason-Goodson's ship. And when next day, still in fair weather, the carrier's sports officer suggested a game of deck hockey between the *Chargers* and the *Veracitys*, and Cameron agreed heartily, he and Grey took no part in it other than to act as cheer leaders.

And that game of hockey was to be the one and only before the change came in the weather. There was scant warning: the routine weather broadcasts, which came in the naval code, spoke of low pressure coming in from westerly but there was no special alarm. The barometric pressure as reported to the Captain by the Special Branch sub-lieutenant appointed for meteorological duties was fairly steady though it had dropped a little since the evening before. But in advance of the weather striking the carrier there were disquieting manifestations from Captain Mason-Goodson.

3

ONE OF those who had been killed at the 4-inch had been the ship's gunnery officer, an RNVR lieutenant. Mason-Goodson spoke of this death to Cameron after the bodies, sewn into their canvas shrouds – in the case of ratings these shrouds were the hammocks in which they had slept in life – had been eased from the planks, eased from under the White Ensign into the North Atlantic's cold anonymity.

'Not much use,' Mason-Goodson said. 'Lacking power of command, don't you know. In fact I'd have relieved him of his duties had God not done so ahead of me.'

Cameron remained silent; there was nothing he could say, but his dislike of Mason-Goodson grew. Mason-Goodson went on, 'Feller wasn't out of the top drawer, that's the point. Few of my officers are, I regret to say. However – there we are, he's dead and that's that. I'm going to requisition your gunner, Cameron. What's his name?'

'Mr Fielder, sir.'

'At least he's RN, should know his stuff. I want him to take over as my gunnery officer for the remainder of the passage.'

'That's an order, sir?'

'Order?' Mason-Goodson stared. 'Damn it, man, of course it's an order! Do I understand you're querying my order?'

Cameron hesitated. 'I was simply wondering about the validity . . . I mean, Mr Fielder isn't borne on the books of *Charger* – none of us are. The party is my responsibility – '

'And I am the Captain of this ship. God has removed one of my officers. God has handily provided another in his place. God's orders are as valid as my own, Cameron, and you will do as you are told.'

'Aye, aye, sir,' Cameron said. He saluted and left the bridge, wondering if he had heard aright.

Chief Petty Officer Malting had been relieved to find that the warrant officer first seen back at Albert Harbour in Greenock was a gunner and not a gunner (T). He would face no undue interference from that quarter. He remained the torpedo expert. Gunners concerned themselves primarily with the guns and if they arsed about too much around the tubes then a canny torpedo-gunner's mate or torpedo-coxswain could bring into play that brain-baffling bullshit that he'd thought about earlier. In any case Mr Fielder seemed a decent sort; they'd had a few talks together. Fielder hadn't had his warrant very long; his last seagoing draft had been chief gunner's mate in the battleship *Queen Elizabeth*, flagship of the Mediterranean Fleet. He'd been aboard the *QE* when she'd been attacked by Eyeties carrying limpet mines when she'd been at anchor in Alexandria harbour, and had settled on the bottom, main deck more or less awash. He spoke of that and of days pre-war in various parts of the world – Hong Kong, Shanghai and Wei-hai-Wei, known to naval men as Wee-i. He spoke of Singapore, Cape Town, Australian ports, Bermuda; but mostly he spoke of the Mediterranean, of Gibraltar and patrols up to Barcelona in the Spanish Civil War, and of the delights and fleshpots of Malta where the bars were many and the women easy. Strada Stretta, known to the men of the fleet as The Gut, had been Fielder's Mecca. Every other doorway a bar, and above the bars the ladies, if you cared to use the term.

That was not all he spoke of: he spoke of Captain Mason-Goodson. He'd been having words with the *Charger*'s chief bosun's mate. He repeated what he'd been told.

'Buffer says the skipper's got a screw loose. Just between

you and me that is, 'Swain.' 'Swain' was the lower-deck term for torpedo-coxswain.

Malting said, 'And the buffer, like.'

'Eh? Oh – and the buffer, yes.'

'Sealed lips,' Malting said with a grin. 'So what did the buffer reckon, sir?'

'Reckon? I don't know what he reckoned. Just said what he said, that's all.' Mr Fielder paused. 'Said he was bawled out by the skipper just before leaving the Clyde. In full hearing of the hands an' all. To do with the readiness of the seaboat. Skipper said to make sure there was a Bible in the boat's bag. Did you ever, eh?'

Malting grinned and said, 'Go on! Sounds a bit barmy, I will say. So what happened?'

'Buffer said he'd never heard of a Bible in a boat's bag. Maybe he didn't use quite the right tone o' voice . . . skipper went mad. Shouted a lot . . . buffer didn't quite get it all. Something about him being the King's representative on board, and the King being head o' the Church of England and thus God's representative on earth, British earth anyway, which made *him* God's representative.'

'Made who?'

'Skipper,' Fielder said briefly.

'So the skipper, he reckons he's God?'

'By proxy like.'

Malting blew out his breath. 'Then we'd best all watch out eh, sir?'

'Never a truer word, 'Swain, never a truer word.'

Malting reckoned it wasn't good for discipline. Officers didn't bawl out chief POs in front of ratings. Not if they were the right sort of officer. And never mind God.

Captain Mason-Goodson scanned the decoded weather report, and listened to the interpretation given by the Met officer, whom he didn't trust an inch. Some weeks earlier, when the ship had been based at Rothesay, spending a period as training carrier for the makee-learn Fleet Air Arm pilots

25

from RNAS Ayr and Machrihanish to practise deck landings, the Met officer had come to him with a report of heavy rain. He had at once made a signal cancelling that day's exercise up and down the Firth of Clyde, an exercise that would have had the ship turning endlessly into wind for the convenience of flyers for whom he, Mason-Goodson, didn't give a fig; flyers were seldom gentlemen and were an ill-disciplined lot that gave a ship a bad name. When later Mason-Goodson had gone out on deck he found a brilliant, rainless day of sun with the Clyde as blue as the Mediterranean. He had bawled the Met officer out but had never discovered why the useless fool had reported rain. This was just as well. The Met officer had gone to his bunk in the early hours as tight as a drum, had woken with a sick headache as part of a monumental hangover, had in accordance with his usual custom made his way to the starboard for'ard sponson to peer at the weather and had found what he'd taken to be rain but had in fact been the result of a practical joke perpetrated by the gunnery officer now deceased: a bucket of water had been unkindly poured over the walkway running above the sponson and this water had descended through the gratings like a violent rainstorm just as the Met man had gone through the door from the hangar deck.

Now Mason-Goodson said, 'Barometer steady. I don't trust the experts farther than I can throw them. A useless bunch, sitting on their backsides in some safe haven ashore. When I first went to sea we didn't get any damn weather reports, we formed our own judgment by looking at the sky and *feeling* the wind.'

'Yes, sir.'

Mason-Goodson looked at the sub-lieutenant suspiciously. 'What d'you mean, yes, sir? You haven't the faintest idea . . . you've been brought up on the new ideas, all technics.'

'Yes, sir,' the Met officer said again.

'All modern ideas are rubbish. Remember that.'

'I will, sir.' The sub-lieutenant was dismissed. He saluted the Captain's already turned back and left the bridge. A little later, however, Commander Warren could be heard issuing orders to the first lieutenant, who passed them on to the chief bosun's mate: the slips and strops on the bower anchors were to be checked, as were the securing wires on the tightly packed aircraft in the hangar. Just in case? Or because Mason-Goodson had taken another look at the sky and had 'felt' the wind?

It would be very many days yet before the carrier reached the Virginia Capes but Mr Trimby, in his cabin, was already starting a letter to his wife, a letter of some sort of explanation together with a hint of an apology for an unfortunate misunderstanding. That was the intent, anyway. But as he struggled with pen and paper Mr Trimby was forced to recognize the inherent impossibility of explaining satisfactorily how it had come about that his trousers were around his ankles and his sister-in-law had stepped out of her knickers. It had to come down to a misunderstanding of intent, which must form the basis of the explanation itself.

Mr Trimby racked his brains.

A trouser repair of some urgency? That still wouldn't explain the knickers. Same applied to, say, a sudden violent itch on his backside; the long arm of coincidence would be wrenched out of its socket if the sister-in-law had simultaneously felt an itch too, although Mr Trimby had read somewhere about the theory of transfer of pain, at any rate between mother and child, mother feeling the pain when the kid broke its arm, that sort of thing.

It was no good.

A clean breast, an abject apology for letting his lust get the better of his common sense? Well – maybe. But not just yet. An idea might come. Shipmates of past years had got out of situations just as tricky, that was if their stories were to be believed. Mr Trimby, who had got no further than 'My dearest darling wife', ripped the paper up and climbed the myriad ladders to the flight deck. He noted that the wind was increasing from the west and that waves were starting to form with white crests, superimposing themselves on the long North Atlantic swell. It was also very cold and Mr Trimby went below again and settled himself into a chair in the wardroom. When stand easy was piped, the bar was opened and Mr Trimby bought himself a gin and lime. Gin might start the thought processes going. But all Mr Trimby was able to think about was his sister-in-law without her knickers.

At three bells in the afternoon watch Mason-Goodson ordered a suprise alteration of course. Before altering, he had initiated an exchange of signals between himself and the senior officer of the escort. The escort leader had demurred; their orders for the Virginia Capes had been unequivocal and any alteration would be in direct contravention. This was overruled by Mason-Goodson, who was the most senior officer on the spot. Thus the carrier and her destroyer escort altered course to starboard, an almost ninety-degree turn northwards towards Iceland and the Denmark Strait, which was patrolled by the armed merchant cruisers of the Northern Patrol. Theirs was a thankless task, endlessly steaming up and down the bitter seas mainly under driving snow at this time of the year, with ice forming blocks around the guns and along the standing rigging and on the decks themselves, turning the latter into skating rinks for the hands as they carried out their duties or relieved the guns' crews and watchkeepers, keeping one hand on the life-lines rigged fore and aft.

As the chief yeoman of signals came down from the bridge to the petty officers' mess, Malting asked him, why the alteration?

'God knows, mate – and I reckon maybe 'e does too.'

'Eh? Come again, Yeo?'

The reply was terse. 'Skipper's got his antennae rigged.'

'Antennae?'

'Skipper's in direct touch.'

Malting recalled what Mr Fielding had reported, that conversation with the buffer. 'Got a nudge, has he, from aloft like?'

The chief yeoman chucked his cap into the corner of a settee and called out to the messman. 'Cup o' char, Stanley.' He cocked an eye at Malting, who nodded. 'Correction: *two* cups.' Then he answered the torpedo-coxswain's question. 'Call it a hunch. I heard him bawling at the navvy,' he said in reference to the navigating officer. 'Something about a ship that's maybe needing assistance up north. Something about a wireless message, but when I checked with the PO Tel 'e was being tight-lipped . . . maybe on orders. But the impression I got was . . . well, that the message hadn't come from any WT aerial.'

'You got that impression from what the skipper was saying?'

The chief yeoman nodded. 'Yes, sort of, I dunno.' There was a reflective look in his eye as the cups of tea were brought by the messman. He lit a cigarette and blew smoke. Then he went on, 'Denmark Strait, that's where we're heading, I reckon. Denmark Strait.'

'Where the *Hood* went.'

'That's just it. Skipper had a nephew in the *Hood*. Paymaster midshipman. I know, see, because I was serving with him in the old *Berwick*. Buzz was that the skipper went on a bundle on the lad – no sprogs of his own, so like a son to him.' He paused. 'Mustn't shoot me mouth off, but. . . .'

'But you're saying – '

'I'm not really saying anything, mate. Just that it's all a bit funny like, what with the God talk an' that. Like he's . . . seen a ghost. Or going round the twist.'

Malting said nothing. The conversation lapsed. They drank their tea. The carrier was rolling badly now, having come broadside to the wind from the west. Malting was thoughtful; it wasn't propitious, not in wartime in mid-Atlantic, to be steaming at a tangent to their orders, at the whim of a captain who saw ghosts and was maybe going clean round the bend. Like Harpic.

The chief yeoman had not been so far from the truth, or

something like it. Captain Mason-Goodson, the night before, had suffered a nightmare after turning in in his sea cabin for a spell, leaving his ship in the hands of the Officer of the Watch, an RNR lieutenant who had proved that he was a capable seaman even if no more a gentleman than Mason-Goodson's other officers. Mason-Goodson had been dead tired, virtually out on his feet after having scarcely left the bridge since leaving the Tail o' the Bank. He had tossed and turned restlessly in the stuffy atmosphere of the small sea-cabin. His mind, after he had fallen asleep, had gone round in circles. He had so much to worry about, as had any captain at sea. Fifteen thousand tons of valuable ship, some five hundred lives now added to by the commissioning party for the *Veracity*. His after 4-inch mounting a semi wreck and many men dead – pity about that, but of course seamen expected to die in wartime, it was what they were paid for and they couldn't really complain. A useless bunch of officers, mostly RNVR from all sorts of curious backgrounds, counter-jumpers, solicitors, clerks, ex-public schoolboys (not Dartmouth) still wet behind the ears . . . they were so many rods for the back of a four-ring captain RN who had been through the mill from naval cadet to his present rank and authority. Not an easy mill until he had become the senior sub-lieutenant aboard the old battleship *Emperor of India* and as such Sub of the Gunroom, a mighty position from which he could rule the snotties with a rod of iron and another of cane to be applied as often as an excuse could be found to their backsides. Caning made men of them, Mason-Goodson knew that as a fact. He had made two of them so manly that they had outstripped him in rank, now flying their flags as rear-admirals commanding cruiser squadrons. That, he had not liked; but the Service was the Service and you had to take the rough with the smooth.

Tossing and turning, seeing all manner of things in that troubled sleep, Mason-Goodson had seen his nephew floating in the icy water of the Denmark Strait after the great battle-cruiser *Hood* had succumbed to the guns of the *Bismark* and the *Prinz Eugen*. Until now the largest warship in the world at

42,100 tons, and gone with only three survivors of whom his nephew had not been one. The news had been a very bad blow. The boy's mother, Mason-Goodson's sister, had naturally been distraught, had even asked Mason-Goodson if he believed Robert's spirit was hovering overhead, trying to communicate, trying perhaps to say goodbye.

Waking with that floating image in his mind, it had taken Mason-Goodson some while to come through the mists to normality. The nightmare, the vicarious struggles for life, had been extremely real and vivid, almost as though he had been present himself or had been watching a film of the catastrophe. Once fully awake he had realized that it had been no more than an appalling dream, a figment of his imagination as the result of the long strain of war and responsibility and the constant pin-pricks of having to deal with temporary officers in whom he had no confidence. Nothing more than that – of course. But the seeming reality of the experience left something behind it.

The transmission of a message, some contact with the power behind the universe? It could be. A contact to make him aware that someone, some ship, somewhere in the vicinity of where the mighty *Hood* had been blown to fragments, might be in need of assistance.

Mason-Goodson felt this very strongly indeed. Returning to the bridge as dawn action stations were sounded by bugle over the Tannoy, Mason-Goodson, duffel-coated against the bitter cold, had brooded over his thoughts throughout the forenoon watch; and that afternoon he had come to his decision. No more time would be wasted. He had ordered the northward alteration towards the Denmark Strait. The navigating officer had demurred, agreeing with the reaction of the escort leader. Mason-Goodson, unwilling to admit his reasons, had snapped back, something about a message. There was to be no argument; he had given his orders and that was that. Speed was increased, the Lieutenant-Commander (E) being ordered to squeeze out extra revolutions. The lookouts were double-banked and threats were uttered as to dire punishment if any men failed to spot anything before the Captain did so.

As the first dog-watchmen relieved the afternoon watch, Cameron was sent for to report to the bridge.

Mason-Goodson said, 'None of my officers has experience of the far northern waters. That's to say, the Denmark Strait. What about your party, Cameron?'

'I've been on Russian convoys myself, sir.'

'Murmansk, Archangel?'

'Yes, sir.'

'But not by way of the Denmark Strait?'

'No, sir. We made our northing east of Iceland.'

'Yes, quite. However, you may be of some use I suppose. I require you to remain on the bridge until further orders, Cameron.'

'Aye, aye, sir.' Cameron hesitated. There was something odd about the Captain's manner. He risked a question. 'What will my orders be, sir?'

'To do as I've just said.'

'Yes, sir. But in what way can I be of help?'

'I don't know yet.' Mason-Goodson moved his shoulders irritably. 'It depends, that's all you need to know.'

There was no answer to that. Cameron caught the eye of the navigating officer behind the Captain's back. Lieutenant-Commander Anderson was RNR, a solid, phlegmatic man who had spent the pre-war years in liners of the Orient Line running to Australia. A no-nonsense man . . . he shrugged, and rolled his eyeballs upward. It was not reassuring. Obviously, Mason-Goodson had had a dispute with his navigator. Cameron felt a sense of unease, almost of foreboding. Another thing was fairly obvious when one read as it were between the lines: Mason-Goodson was taking his ship off her course without orders from the Admiralty. Even more obvious was the certainty that Mason-Goodson would not be reporting his deviation to the home command: you didn't break wireless silence at sea in wartime.

Obeying orders, Cameron remained on the bridge, feeling

like nothing more than a spare hand. Mason-Goodson hunched himself on his stool on the port side of the small bridge, behind the glass screen, and stared out ahead. Snow began to fall, whitened the bridge personnel, had constantly to be wiped from the glass of the gyro repeater in the binnacle. Anderson and Cameron talked in low voices. Mason-Goodson spoke without looking round. 'Stop that damn chatter. Like a couple of schoolgirls. . . . We all need to be alert, and to concentrate.'

Anderson said, 'It would help if we knew what on, sir.'

There was a longish pause, then Mason-Goodson let drop the first clue. Still without turning to face them he said, 'Someone may stand in need of us, pilot.'

Once again Cameron and the navigator exchanged looks. Solemn-faced, Anderson lifted a gloved hand and touched the fingers against his forehead.

Like Warrant Engineer Trimby, Chief PO Malting was writing an instalment of the letter to his wife which he would post on arrival in Norfolk, Virginia. Every day at sea since the start of the war, or anyway when duty and action permitted, he had written such an instalment. Much of what he wrote had to do with the running of the pub because, even though the licensing justices and the brewery had permitted the transfer of the licence to Bessie in his absence, he still couldn't really believe that any woman, even Bessie who was as tough as an oak tree, could run a pub successfully. So his letters always contained a lot of unwanted advice. There was always a sentence or two, daily, about how much he loved Bessie but there had been so many days of war already, and inspiration for variations of expression didn't come easily, with the result that there was a lot of repetition. But he knew that women never tired of being told that they were loved so he wrote it down.

Much of the completed letters had to do with their perennial problem: their daughter Marianne. Problem was the word, all right. Marianne was rising seventeen and Ben

Malting and Bessie had to face it, she was a proper little tart. Painted face, peroxided hair, breasts and nipples made the most of by tight bodices or whatever it was women wore in that region, skirts that seemed to ride right up when she sat down and crossed her legs provocatively. Boy friends like bees round a honeypot, and mostly unsuitable even if she'd been the right age for Ben to accept the fact, the eventually inevitable fact, of boy friends of any sort. Ben knew very well that all they wanted was the one thing. He prayed to God they wouldn't get it, and deep down he didn't believe they would, because, horrid though it might be even to think such thoughts of one's own daughter, he fancied Marianne was a prick teaser. Whether she was or not, she was a continuing source of anxiety. Of embarrassment, too. The brewery rep, a sour man of a little beyond middle age and a lay reader at his local church, always eyed her askance and was inclined to click his tongue. Bessie had written that she dreaded what Mr Tomkins might report back to the office. On the other hand – looking on the bright side – Marianne when she could be persuaded to help her mum in the saloon bar was a definite asset to the trade, a real draw. Married chiefs and POs from RNB, dropping in without their wives, had often complimented Bessie on her daughter and it was a rare Saturday night when she didn't get her bottom pinched a couple of times or so, whereupon she would emit a high-pitched giggle that alerted mum and caused the offending hand to be smartly withdrawn. . . .

The day's instalment ended, 'I love you very much dear heart and I hope M. is not giving you no trouble.'

Malting shoved the pad of paper away in his ditty box and left the PO's mess, climbing to the hangar and then up to the port for'ard walkway below the edge of the flight deck. It was dark now, very dark and bitterly cold; without her navigation lights the carrier steamed ghostlike through the murk of the falling snow. She was still rolling quite heavily, a real pregnant duck of a ship, not like the cruisers and destroyers that went through the water like knives, thrusting up great clean bow waves to stream down the sides to port and starboard. Malting shivered; all around them was gloom and murkiness, no light in the heavens, no stars, no moon – and why the boody hell were they steaming north? What had happened, for God's sake? If Cameron had been in command he'd have told the ship's company by now. As it was, nobody knew sod all. The PO's mess had been full of stupid buzzes: they were going into the Denmark Strait to back up the poor buggers of the Northern Patrol, they were under orders for a Russian convoy, going through the dangerous passage to the west of Iceland to join up north of Kautarhotn in the Arctic Circle, they were going to Greenland on a secret mission to pick up Goering who'd chucked his hand in . . . there was never an end to the daftness of the buzzes and there was always someone to believe them unless the skipper set their minds at rest.

Malting sighed and went back inside where it was warmer. The blokes on the bridge would be getting their balls frozen off, he thought. In the hangar he met the ship's buffer, Chief Petty Officer Stoner. Stoner was carrying out another check on the securing wires of the aircraft. He said, 'Wotcha, 'Swain. You look what I might call chokker.'

'It's the big-ship effect,' Malting said. 'That, and being a spare hand most of the time.' He looked around the hangar; when the ship rolled, there seemed to be quite a strain on the wires and he remarked on this, wondering what would happen if any of the wires should part.

'Bloody lash-up, that's what,' Stoner answered. 'We've not been jam-packed like this before, not ever. Normal operational complement is twenty-four aircraft. Now there's no leeway if anything takes charge, runs amok. Not with forty of the buggers.'

Malting listened to the surge of the waves as the westerly wind drove them against the thin plating of the hangar's port side. Every now and again a larger than usual sea passed beneath the carrier, resulting in an almost ten-degree roll, and the whole hangar seemed to drum with the reverberation.

He saw the look of concern on Stoner's face: Stoner was used to carriers, Malting was not, but it was clear enough that Stoner wasn't happy. Remarking that he was going to get the Officer of the Watch to call out the duty hands of the flight deck party, he moved away along the sloping steel deck towards the ladder leading to the navigating bridge in the superstructure. Malting made his way back below to the mess.

Lieutenant-Commander(E) Chatterton, ex-Cunard White Star Line, was well accustomed to the run across the North Atlantic from Southampton to the Ambrose Channel Light Vessel; he was not accustomed to running north, slap across the prevailing westerlies. And he was concerned about his engine-room, which was drumming like the hangar. That of itself didn't worry him, anyway not apart from the fact that the *Charger* had a peculiar motion in a seaway, a motion that was all her own, a nasty sort of twist when she rolled. This twist caused her, now and again, to lift her stern so far that her single screw came clear of the water and began to race. That was never good for any engine, and the carrier was overdue for refit and an engine-room overhaul, which of course – no need to remind himself of it – was why she was going to the States without her Fleet Air Arm squadron embarked. Or had been going to the States; Chatterton had been as amazed as everyone else aboard when the alteration to the north had come. And he didn't like the way the weather was shaping. Had they remained on their westerly course he wouldn't have been unduly worried by the weather; but steaming with worsening conditions on the beam was a different kettle of fish altogether.

Below now on the starting-platform he spoke to his senior engineer. 'I wonder what bee's got into Father's bonnet now.' The Captain, skipper to the lower deck, was Father to the wardroom. 'There has to be a reason. Or I suppose there has.'

The senior engineer didn't respond. In his view there wasn't much you could say about Mason-Goodson that wasn't derogatory, so he refrained from saying it. He'd fallen foul of the Captain from the start, when on joining the ship in the Clyde some months earlier he'd reported as was customary to Mason-Goodson in his cabin and had been told in a supercilious voice that he was scruffy. 'I suggest a clothes-brush for a start,' Mason-Goodson had said, and had gone on to remark that Merchant Service engineers had no right to masquerade as officers. Lieutenant (E) Tapp was not in possession of a full RNR commission: he was on what was known as a T124X agreement under which Merchant Service engineers had been co-opted to serve in certain ships on a temporary basis and had been accorded RNR stripes for the duration of the agreement. Tapp had sailed previously in a collier owned by a tramp company sailing mainly to the Continent from UK ports. They had all been scruffy; and Tapp, not a man to be put down, had come back at Mason-Goodson with the comment that he, Mason-Goodson, might well do himself a favour by dirtying his hands once in a while. Mason-Goodson had ordered him out of his cabin and had had his name entered in the log for impertinence and insubordination. Not a good start, but Tapp couldn't have cared less. All he wanted was for the war to be over so that he could shake the bullshit of the RN for ever off his feet. Now, he informed the chief engineer that he was about to make a routine inspection of the steering engine in the tiller flat.

'Go ahead,' Chatterton said. 'On that article, our lives might well depend – if the weather worsens.'

Later, he was to remember that.

Mason-Goodson, together with the navigating officer and Cameron, remained on the bridge throughout the night. At intervals steaming hot cocoa was brought up from the galley by the bosun's mate of the watch. Cameron drank his gratefully, feeling the warmth as it went down. There was still snow, and the wind had increased, was battering the carrier's port side. As the ship rolled heavily to starboard, Cameron looked straight down into the water as it rose almost to the bridge itself. That bridge seemed to him to have been an afterthought, stuck onto the starboard side of the flight deck to hang clear of the hull, directly over the water, supported by two thick stanchions rising from above the sponson. The ship gave him the feeling of being something of a hermaphrodite. His knowledge of aircraft-carriers was slight enough but he believed the escort carriers had been laid down as merchant ships – that in fact they had merchant ship hulls, built to carry cargo, and had had an aircraft-carrier as it were superimposed onto them under the exigencies of war and the enormous and very welcome assistance that the United States was making to Britain. The result, or so Cameron felt, was a vessel stitched together rather than constructed as a whole from the start. He was finding this disturbing; the sooner he could reach the Norfolk naval base and take over command of his own destroyer, the better. . . .

At last there were signs of dawn in the eastern sky.

'It's lightening, sir,' the navigator said to the Captain's back, half expecting to find that Mason-Goodson had drifted off into a cat-nap.

Not so. 'God's light,' Mason-Goodson said.

'Yes, sir. Maybe something'll show. Whatever it is we're looking for.'

'He may show us, certainly.'

'Who may, sir?'

'God, of course.'

Anderson said, 'Yes, of course.' He paused. 'May I know, sir, how long you propose to maintain our present course?'

'I don't know yet, pilot. It's in God's hands.'

'I hope He'll decide soon in that case. In my opinion we should be altering back to the west. I don't like the way the ship's handling.'

'Kindly don't argue, navigator.'

Anderson let out a long breath of sheer frustration. 'It's not a case of arguing, sir. I'm stating my view as your navigator. The ship is obviously labouring and the weather's worsening. If we don't soon head into the wind and sea we might find it's too late to make the turn. If we broach to – '

'We shall not broach to.'

'Oh, for God's sake, sir – '

'Do not speak of God in that way, navigator.' Angrily, the Captain swung round. 'I shall not tolerate blasphemy in my presence. Is that quite clearly understood?'

'It was not intended as blasphemy, sir. But I repeat what I warned you of. With respect, sir. I have crossed the Atlantic a damn sight more times than you have and I don't like the feel of things as they are. We've already made too much northing in the prevailing conditions, and – ' He broke off: an Aldis lamp was winking from the senior officer of the destroyer escort. The Yeoman of the Watch read off the signal and reported to the Captain.

'Object on the port bow, sir, bearing one-oh degrees, appears to be a seaboat.'

All eyes looked out on the bearing. Mason-Goodson had heaved himself up from his stool and was staring through his binoculars and the falling snow. Cameron saw what he believed was indeed a boat, a boat under oars, rising and falling on the disturbed surface, lost to view as it went down into the troughs, visible again as it rose on the crests.

Mason-Goodson said, 'God has answered. Give that boat a lee, pilot.'

4

As THE carrier closed towards the open boat, coming round to put her bulk between the wind and the castaways, Cameron saw through his binoculars the bodies strewn in unnatural positions across the thwarts and on the bottom boards. The boat had clearly been overloaded; there were around thirty men aboard her, Cameron fancied. It was a miracle of a sort that the boat hadn't capsized. It looked soggy, as dead as its occupants appeared to be, and the gunwales stood only just clear of the water. But as Anderson brought the carrier to within three cables'-lengths of the boat, Cameron saw an arm waving from the mass of bodies, and another man by the tiller showing signs of life. Soon after this, a seaboat was seen making across with difficulty from the destroyer leader.

Captain Mason-Goodson turned round again, called for the bosun's mate.

'Here, sir – '

'A message to the first lieutenant. He's to take away the seaboat and assist. Pipe the seaboat's crew and lowerers.'

'Aye, aye, sir.'

The bosun's mate went down the ladder to the wheelhouse below the bridge, moving at the rush. A few moments later the Tannoy broadcast throughout the ship, mustering the seaboat's crew and lowerers of the watch. As the men ran for the seaboat's falls, Malting was on the starboard for'ard walkway with Petty Officer Berridge.

'Suicide,' he said.

Berridge nodded. The sea always meant sacrifice; always had. You didn't hang back when someone was in trouble. As they watched in growing concern the boat from the destroyer came into view. Just for an instant. Then a big sea drove right under her, and lifted her to hang poised briefly on its crest, and then the boat was seen to slide down the wave into the boiling trough, spilling lifejacketed men like crumbs of bread thrown to seagulls. Heads bobbed about, but quickly vanished from sight as the bulky carrier completed her turn for the purpose of shielding the semi-derelict boatload.

Malting said, 'I dunno if God was concerned, Archie.'

'Eh?'

'What the buffer said about the skipper's notions. Answering a heavenly call. I don't reckon God would take a half-dozen lives in exchange for what might be alive in that boat. Eh?'

There didn't seem to be an answer to that.

The carrier's seaboat, an American-built whaler, was got away, the falls slipped on the crest of a wave. In a trice the seaboat, with the first lieutenant embarked, all the crew wearing heavy cork lifejackets, was half a cable's-length clear of the ship. Rising to the crests, falling to the troughs and coming up again, pulled manfully by the soaked but sweating seamen towards the dangerously overloaded boat. The distance thereafter closed only very slowly as, coming out from the immediate lee of the carrier's big hull, the full force of the storm took them, battered at them, shrieking like a multitude of demons, driving the snow into their bodies, searching beneath the oilskins and duffel-coats and sou'westers. Layton, the carrier's first lieutenant, an RNR officer of long experience, urged them on, encouraging, exhorting, keeping them pulling hard at the oars with every ounce of their strength as the raging sea tossed them around like a cork. As they rose to yet another crest a boat was seen pulling across from the *Invermore*, making way slowly. Both boats edged nearer the spilled men from the first seaboat. Two men were seen in the water, held on the disturbed surface by the lifejackets; both were lying with their heads down in the water, their arms hanging limp. Layton saw them: dead, succumbed to the terrible cold coming down from the Denmark Strait.

There was worse to come. As the *Charger*'s seaboat neared its target, it was taken by an immense sea, rose upwards at grotesque speed and then, as it went down into the trough, Layton saw the other boat lying immediately beneath. There was nothing he could do. His boat came down hard and fast on the boatload of survivors, smashing right on top of it, splintering woodwork, crushing men, the living with the dead. It was total destruction.

There was signalling from the senior officer of the escort; the *Invermore*'s seaboat, closing the disaster a matter of minutes after the smash, had picked up a man. Just one man, and he was alive if only just, but he'd managed to speak. In English, although he was Greek, chief officer of a Greek tramp ship sailing independently south through the Denmark Strait where it had been attacked by a German surface raider and sunk. It was assumed that the boat had contained all the survivors from the attack.

Captain Mason-Goodson took in the information; the yeoman waited, deferentially. Mason-Goodson snapped, 'Well, what is it, Yeoman?'

'Senior officer, sir. Asks for orders, sir.'

Mason-Goodson seemed undecided. Anderson said sourly, 'God's done enough for today if you want my opinion, sir.'

'I do not, thank you. I've warned you before about blasphemy. Your name will be entered in the log.'

Anderson gave a short laugh. 'Thy will be done.'

Mason-Goodson swung away angrily without responding, though Cameron knew he must have heard. He passed his orders to the yeoman. 'Make, *Invergarry* from *Charger*, am altering south-westerly to resume passage for Norfolk.'

A long breath of relief came from the navigator. Without waiting for the Captain's order, he passed the word down to the quartermaster in the wheelhouse. 'Port ten, engine to full ahead.'

'Port ten, telegraph to full ahead, sir.' There was a pause, then: 'Ten o' port wheel on, sir, telegraph repeated full ahead.'

'And may God be with us all,' Anderson said in a voice that he made no effort to keep low. Within the next half-minute the carrier began her swing into and then across the wind and sea, rolling badly as the full force of what was now not far off a full gale took her exposed starboard bow. Steadying as the helm came off at Anderson's next order, she steamed south-westerly. Without her first lieutenant, without the seaboat's crew of the port watch.

That afternoon, another of her executive officers was injured. An RNVR sub-lieutenant lost his footing at the head of a steel ladder leading from the officers' cabin flat to the hangar. Crashing out of control as the ship gave a sudden heavy lurch, he went flat on the deck some twelve feet below, twisting as he fell. He came down on a ringbolt in the deck. The surgeon lieutenant-commander reported a broken back. The prognosis was not good. The young officer died during the night.

'Ship's got a jonah aboard,' Grey said. Cameron had at last been relieved of Mason-Goodson's requirement of him on the bridge and was relaxing in the wardroom. 'Gunnery officer, first lieutenant, seaboat's crew . . . and now this. Three guesses as to who the jonah is.'

'Insubordination,' Cameron said with a grin. 'Your name'll be entered in the log.'

Grey said, 'How well *that* would read at the Admiralty!' He mimicked the hypothetical log entry. 'Had occasion this day to reprimand Temporary Lieutenant Neil Harold Grey, Royal Naval Reserve, in that he did slanderously state that I was a jonah.' He laughed, but there was no humour in it.

There was an unhealthy feeling throughout the ship now, a feeling of no confidence in the Captain. This, Cameron thought, was not entirely fair. Mason-Goodson's curious, God-inspired hunch had proved no red herring after all. The boatload of dead and dying had been no mirage, and a life had been saved, and more would have been saved but for an unfortunate accident of the sea. But at a price . . . and unfair or not, the feeling amongst the ship's company was real and had to be accepted as an unwelcome fact. Messmates who that morning had been alive and looking forward to the fleshpots of America were now dead. Mason-Goodson had defied orders in altering for the Denmark Strait and those messmates had died because of it. The feeling in the wardroom was similar: Layton had been a good first lieutenant, and popular with it. He had a wife and two young children. His home was outside Liverpool, but he'd had the family up to Rothesay on the Isle of Bute when the carrier had been engaged in deck-landing training. They'd stayed at the Victoria Hotel, right opposite the pier where the libertyboats from the aircraft-carriers and the submarines of the 7th Submarine Flotilla had disembarked their shore-going personnel. The officers used to foregather in the bar of the Victoria Hotel and had come to know and like Layton's wife, Jennifer. Layton had brought the family aboard once or twice, and once Mason-Goodson, in an unusual fit of understanding, had allowed the children, two boys, to remain aboard for a day's exercises in the Firth of Clyde. There were memories aboard of those two boys, now fatherless, standing at the fore end of the flight deck to watch their father taking charge of the operation of weighing anchor.

Along the messdecks as the carrier pushed south-westerly through the worsening weather to rejoin her ordered track for the Virginia Capes, there was talk. Leading hands of messes talked of organizing auctions of the dead men's gear once the ship was berthed in Norfolk. At such messdeck auctions extravagant sums were bid and the proceeds sent to the families ashore in the UK. Ridiculously large sums were raised in the case of popular messmates. The lower deck was tightly knit and looked after its own.

Other talk was of Mason-Goodson. The yarn about his hunch, or his vision if you cared to look on it as that, had spread. The skipper had invoked God. Not necessarily a bad thing to do, and there were many occasions when the most hardened, most foul-mouthed and most boozy of seamen had prayed at times of danger, prayed for last-minute forgiveness for sins past. But you could not make decisions at sea on the basis of a personal message from the Almighty: to do so smacked of Adolf Hitler, who had also had messages from God. It was understood that Hitler had been advised by heavenly contact not to invade the UK after the debacle at Dunkirk, when the British Army had been ripped apart and the coasts stood wide open to invasion, with Winston nattering on about fighting on the beaches and never surrendering. That had been the worst ever bloomer on Adolf's part. Maybe God had made adverse signals by intent, in which case He really was on the British side.

In any case the general opinion on the messdecks was that the skipper was going barmy.

On the bridge during the middle watch that night the Officer of the Watch called down the voice-pipe to the Captain's sea-cabin.

Mason-Goodson came awake as soon as he heard the whistle. 'Yes, what is it?'

'Roll's increasing, sir.'

'Badly?'

'I'd say so, sir. The inclinometer's showing fifteen degrees at times.'

'Wind speed?'

'Ninety knots, sir. And gusts above that.'

'I'm coming up. Call the navigator.' The voice-pipe cover was snapped shut. On the bridge the Officer of the Watch put back the cover at his end. The bridge stood around ninety feet above the sea but heavy spray was sweeping over the fo'c'sle and the fore end of the flight deck, and was reaching the bridge. The cold struck through layer after layer of clothing – duffel-coat, oilskin, thick woollen sweater, gloves, scarf. There was no let-up. Mason-Goodson reached the bridge within half a minute, to be followed by Lieutenant-Commander Anderson.

'Well, pilot. What do you think?'

'Time we turned westerly, sir.'

'Damn it, pilot, we're not down to our track yet!'

'Does that matter?'

'Matter?' Mason-Goodson glared through the spray and the driven snow. The weather froze men's faces, was as painful as the blow of a fist. 'Of course it matters. It matters because I say so.'

'Oh. I see, sir. What you say is more important than the safety of the ship.' Anderson turned to the Officer of the Watch. 'How long has it been like this, Jenkins?'

'Not long, sir. Wind worsened just a few minutes ago, so I called the – '

'Yes, all right.' Anderson addressed the Captain again. 'I consider the ship to be in danger, sir. We should turn forty-five degrees to starboard immediately, to head into wind and sea – '

'I have just said – '

'I know what you've just said, sir, and in my opinion that was lunatic bollocks. If we hold our course we're likely to broach to.' Anderson paused, then went on, 'If you don't give the order yourself I shall give it.'

Mason-Goodson waved a fist in the navigator's face. 'That would constitute an act of mutiny, God damn you!'

Anderson said, 'A lesser risk, I fancy, than leaving the ship where she is. Will you please give the order, sir, and save a lot of unpleasantness as well as lives?'

Mason-Goodson fumed. 'Your conduct will be reported to the Admiralty with a view to Court Martial the moment we reach the USA.'

'I'll risk that too,' Anderson said.

In a voice as cold as the snow itself, as cold as the ice forming on the bridge from the spray, Mason-Goodson gave the order.

Below in his cabin, lying awake and listening to the sounds of the sea battering at the thin side of the carrier alongside his bunk, hearing the drumming from the hangar as waves swept the flight deck and the sea poured down onto what was left of the 4-inch mountings aft, Cameron immediately felt the effect of the alteration of course. The carrier still rolled but also began to pitch as her stem bit into the waves, rose to them and fell again. The roll itself was less than before, much less, while the pitch, if uncomfortable, was unimportant; and the sounds of the ship's agony were muted now. Cameron sent up his own vote of thanks to a provident God, who seemed to have put some sense into Mason-Goodson's mind at last. Cameron had had the feeling very strongly that the ship had been in danger of breaking up. It had been no business of his as a mere passenger aboard a ship of which he had had no previous experience; and he knew that the navigating officer wouldn't allow it to come to that. Cameron had seen for himself that Anderson stood in no awe of Mason-Goodson and didn't draw back from speaking his mind when he saw the need. So long as Anderson was there, they would come through.

He drifted off at last to sleep. At three bells in the morning watch his steward brought a cup of tea.

'Good morning, sir. Good filthy morning I should say, sir.'

'It feels it,' Cameron said, yawning and stretching. 'But she's riding better than she was earlier.'

'Not before time, sir. Chief steward's lost half his pantry ware.'

'How about the aircraft?'

There was a grin. 'Not on the chief steward's requisition, sir, them lot. Me, I only commute between the pantry and the cabins, sir.'

Cameron had heard no sounds from above that might

indicate any of the aircraft parting their securing wires and taking charge. No doubt all was well in the hangar. He was drinking his tea when the bridge messenger knocked on his cabin bulkhead and drew the curtain aside.

'Captain's compliments, sir, and he'd like to see you on the bridge.'

The Captain's wishes were an order. Cameron dressed as quickly as he could.

Mason-Goodson turned as Cameron said, 'Captain, sir. You wished to see me.'

'Yes. You've taken your time, Cameron.'

'I'm sorry, sir.'

'Well, never mind. But I trust you move faster in action. Now – owing to the casualties I'm short of executive officers, watchkeepers. You haven't understudied as I wished, but you'll have to do the best you can. I require you and your better officers to help out with the bridge watchkeeping. Understood, Cameron?'

'Yes, sir.'

'Good. Contact my senior watchkeeper and draw up a rota.'

'Aye, aye, sir.' Cameron waited; there might be more to come and there was, of a sort.

'That's all, Cameron. Except that you're unshaven. See to it immediately.'

Cameron saluted and turned away down the ladder. It would be courting danger uselessly to point out to Mason-Goodson that shaving would have taken up yet more time. Possibly he expected his officers to be at all times shaven ready for a summons to his presence.

For some while now all personnel had been ordered by Tannoy to keep off the upper deck, which aboard a carrier meant, effectively, the flight deck but included the open after deck and the fo'c'sle. These would be visited only under direct orders from the bridge, and such orders would be given only in an emergency. The bridge watchkeepers – Officer of the Watch, signal staff, bosun's mate and messenger – could reach their stations via the ladder from the hangar to flying control abaft the bridge and the bridge itself. Likewise the quartermaster and telegraphsman in the wheelhouse. Until an emergency arose there was no need for any of the ship's company to expose himself to danger. In current conditions the armament, now effectively down to the sixteen 40mm close-range guns mounted on sponsons and along the walkways, was not being manned. In such seas no U-boat could operate; such as might be around would have gone well beneath periscope depth, riding out the gale's ferocity in comparative calm below. Similarly there would be no threat from the air; in any case they were by now outside the range of the Focke-Wulfs that harassed the convoys while they were closer to the Western Approaches. For now, Hitler's various armadas were not the chief worry.

The enemy was the weather. In peace or war, the weather could be an enemy every bit as lethal as the Nazis.

And as full dark came down that day the order to remain below was flouted by one of the ship's officers, a lieutenant of the depleted bridge watchkeeping rota. It was done with the best of intentions; he'd attempted to save an innocent feline life. Crossing the hangar he had, or so it was assumed, looked upwards and had seen the ship's cat making its way along a walkway leading to the alleyway that ran past the Captain's quarters immediately below the flight deck. He must have gone in pursuit – no one knew for certain why. He had perhaps felt the weather coming into the hangar: the door leading into the walkway on the port side near the Captain's quarters had later been found to be open. Through this door the cat could have exited onto the flight deck. All that had been known for certain was the lieutenant had been seen staggering about on the flight deck, buffeted by the wind and the sea coming solid over the fore end of the deck. Cameron, taking his first spell as a co-opted watchkeeper, had made the sighting and had at once ordered the searchlight in flying control to be switched on. The beam had swept the flight deck; the cat, its fur laid flat by the seawater, had been seen clinging for its life to one of the trip-wires running across the deck. Green eyes, catching the searchlight's beam, had stared in desperation towards the bridge. Then, as Cameron watched, the young lieutenant was taken by an extra heavy gust of tearing wind that filled his oilskin like a sail and carried him willy-nilly towards the walkway and straight over the carrier's side into the boiling, murderous sea.

There was nothing to be done. To turn the ship now would be disastrous. It was imperative to hold her head to the wind and sea. Mason-Goodson was informed, and came to the bridge.

'Who was it?' he asked.

It was the bosun's mate of the watch who gave the answer, naming the lost officer.

'Bloody fool,' Mason-Goodson said furiously. 'What about the damn cat?'

'Still there, sir,' Cameron said.

'And there,' Mason-Goodson said, tight-lipped, 'it damn well remains. Any man who goes after it will be placed in cells. Or shot. The blasted animal's deprived me of another watchkeeper.'

He was, of course, quite right. No more lives could be put in jeopardy, so much was obvious. It was the way the Captain had said it that left a nasty taste in Cameron's mouth.

5

It DIDN'T do Mason-Goodson any good at all; the bosun's mate talked. Seamen were sentimental about cats. Every ship had one, and theirs, name of Nelson, had been left to freeze to death. That was an omen. They all knew that the Captain couldn't have ordered its rescue, but somehow that wasn't the point. If the skipper hadn't left the alteration of course too late it might never have happened, the poor wretched moggie might not have decided to go exploring on deck . . . they even recognized the fallacy in this utterance but it made no difference. The skipper, according to the bosun's mate, had spoken nastily about the cat. The young lieutenant now became something of a hero, giving his life to go after Nelson.

It may have been the cat, it may not have been; but within a few hours of the episode the weather did what had seemed impossible: it worsened, and worsened alarmingly.

The wind indicator on the bridge showed gusts of up to 130 knots. And the roll had come back in fullest measure. Everyone on the bridge had to cling on for their lives as the structure swooped to starboard, rose again, and fell back to port, time and again until it felt as though bridge and wheelhouse must be wrenched from their supports. Neil Grey, Cameron's first lieutenant, co-opted by Mason-Goodson, was taking the watch when an alarming din came from below, what seemed to be the sound of tearing metal followed by crashes against the ship's plates.

Mason-Goodson swung round. 'What the devil was that?'

It was the navigator who answered. 'Sounds like the aircraft taking charge,' Anderson said.

'Bosun's mate.'

'Yes, sir?'

'Pipe, all seamen of the watch below to muster in the hangar. At the double. Commander and chief bosun's mate to report to the bridge.'

'Aye, aye, sir.'

The pipe was made. Chief Petty Officer Stoner came to the bridge, sweating despite the cold. His hands dripped blood: they had been torn by the parted wires in the hangar.

'What's going on, Stoner?'

The answer was no surprise. 'Aircraft on the move, sir. Securing wire – '

'Damage?'

'All the lot's going to go, I reckon sir. Maybe started with just one that took off and ran amok, sir. It's a shambles down there, sir.'

'No doubt. I shall have someone's balls for this. Go back and cope, Stoner.'

'Yes, sir.' Stoner hesitated. 'Sir, I reckon – '

'Don't argue with me, Chief Petty Officer Stoner. I'm not interested in what you *reckon*. My order was, go down and cope.'

'Aye, aye, sir.' Stoner saluted and turned away for the ladder. Hidebound old bastard, he was thinking. Callous and uncaring with it. Just like the business of the cat. Stoner had been going to say that to put men into the hangar would be suicidal and pointless. The damage was beyond control, the aircraft were in any case obsolete and after being stripped of any parts worth saving were due to be destroyed after arrival in America. They might just as well be left to destroy themselves where they were, why not? As for coping, you couldn't cope with the humanly impossible.

As Stoner went down towards the hangar he stood aside for

the Commander who was making for the bridge in answer to the Captain's summons. Commander Warren paused for a word, looking down at the chaos.

'Nothing to be done about that, chief, other than take it up on the lifts and dump it – and not before the weather moderates I need hardly add.'

'Yessir – '

'I heard the pipe, chief. Disregard it.'

'Is that an order, sir?'

Warren nodded. 'I'm not having the hands cut to pieces. See that they keep clear. I'll be having a word with the Captain.'

He went on up the ladder, fast, holding tight as the ship lurched heavily to port, rolling her guts out. Just before he made the bridge he became aware of light coming through at intervals from one of the welded seams in the side of the hangar, on the port side. He stopped. The ship was now rolling to starboard; when it came back to port the light vanished. Water came through instead, in massive spurts.

He stared, horrified, for an instant. Then he raised his voice in a shout. '*Stoner!*'

'Yessir. Seen it, sir – '

'If much comes through and gets below, we're going to need the pumps. I'll warn the engine-room from the wheelhouse.' Warren went on up, went into the wheelhouse and took up the sound-powered telephone to the engine-room. Chatterton answered himself from the starting platform. Warren said, 'Welded seam going in the hangar. Water coming through. We'll probably need the pumps.' He rang off and climbed to the bridge.

Mason-Goodson said, 'You took your time, Commander.'

Warren disregarded the rebuke. He said, 'Welded seams giving way, sir. We're in for trouble if it goes any further – '

'In the hangar?'

'Yes, port side – '

'The flight deck party can assist the shipwright, Commander. I assume we're in no immediate danger.'

'I'd not assume that. Once a welded seam starts, it can't be stopped by any flight deck party or shipwright, sir. And I've taken the precaution of holding the hands clear of the chaos in the hangar.'

Mason-Goodson faced the Commander, hands clenched into fists and his face almost purple with anger. 'The devil you have! You realize that's in direct contravention of my own order to the chief bosun's mate – who managed to get to the bridge before you did – '

'Yes, sir, I realize that, but I considered the order to be madness in the circumstances as they are in the hangar.' Warren was having to shout into the Captain's face to make himself heard above the shriek of the wind and the menacing sounds from the hangar. 'I suggest you go below and look for yourself, sir.'

Mason-Goodson was almost dancing with rage. 'I suggest you consider yourself under arrest, Commander – '

'I shall not do so, sir. You don't seem to realize that your ship may be in extreme danger – '

He broke off as there came a whistle from the voice-pipe from the engine-room. Mason-Goodson turned, bent to answer it. The lieutenant-commander(E) was speaking. When he replaced the voice-pipe cover Mason-Goodson seemed a shade uncertain. He said, 'Chatterton reports water reaching the tiller flat. I shall go below, Commander. You'll remain here in my place to act as necessary.'

The threat of arrest seemed to be in abeyance. Warren met the navigating officer's eye, and winked.

Mason-Goodson went down the ladder.

Warren had had little confidence in Mason-Goodson from the start. Mason-Goodson was the most pig-headed captain he'd ever served under. Mason-Goodson had been a gunnery specialist and the gunnery officers were known in the fleet to be rigid-minded and capable of thinking only of the guns, all else passing them by. They tended to think of themselves as the king pins: the whole purpose of the guns was the whole

54

purpose of the ship which was there for the sole purpose of taking the guns to wherever they might be required. All aboard – seamen and stokers, executive and engineer officers, paymasters and writers, cooks and stewards, surgeons and signal staff, the lot – were there for the one reason: to carry the guns. A ship was a floating fortress and nothing else, and if it happened to sink and take the guns down with it, then it was equivalent to an act of mutiny. . . .

Warren believed that Mason-Goodson knew nothing of ship construction; and was certain he knew nothing about aircraft-carriers. He was a dug-out, brought back from retirement at the start of the war. His peacetime appointments after doing his time as a lieutenant had all been in the capital ships – the battleships and battle-cruisers. Ashore, he had commanded the Devonport gunnery school and had gone from there to an appointment that, for his speciality, could only be considered an odd one: he'd been appointed to command the fishery protection flotilla, all small ships. There would have been a reason for such an obscure appointment; but Warren didn't know what it was. He could only make guesses. Probably Mason-Goodson had fallen foul of his seniors. It would never have been hard to fall out with Mason-Goodson. Some eighteen months before the declaration of war, Captain Mason-Goodson had gone onto the retired list without the customary accolade of being promoted to rear-admiral on retirement. There had to be a reason for that as well.

And now *Charger* was stuck with him.

Warren was a very different sort. He was one of those executive officers who believed that seamanship came first in any naval officer's list of priorities. The guns would go to hell if the seamen failed in their duty. Thus he had remained what the navy called a salt horse, an officer who had never specialized – a basic seaman. He happened to be a good one. And he had had a wide and varied experience. Destroyers, cruisers, big-ship time in the *Renown*, a commission in the aircraft-carrier *Hermes*, China side, in the late 1930s. He was not entirely ignorant of aircraft-carriers, their construction, their role in the fleet and their handling.

He was highly apprehensive as to what was going to happen now. The ship couldn't go on taking the storm. The wind had risen to hurricane force, with the spume blown into what looked like a white carpet broken only by the great rearing crests themselves, crests that were all of sixty to seventy feet in height, maybe more. The radar was from time to time reporting echoes of eighty or so feet and in the prevailing conditions those echoes could only have bounced off the waves themselves. God alone, apart from those involved, knew what conditions must be like aboard the escorting destroyers that were visible from time to time, battling through the mountainous seas, climbing the crests to race down again into the troughs.

Warren was very uneasy; from time to time as the ship rolled so heavily to starboard he felt that the bridge super-structure was rolling further than the ship herself. Each time the carrier straightened and then went over to port, Warren fancied there was a jolt, as though the bridge had re-established contact with the hull. He remarked on this to Anderson. Anderson had felt it as well. He'd reported it to the Captain, he said.

'And his response?'

'Just said it was imagination. An over-wrought one, he said. Never exactly polite, is Father.'

'No action taken?'

'No action taken.'

'I'll get the shipwright onto it,' Warren said.

Anderson grinned. 'Without a word to Father, sir?'

'That's right.'

Mason-Goodson returned to the bridge from his investigations below. 'A lot of damn fuss about nothing,' he said, sounding angry. 'Very little water entering, seam not widening . . . no more than a slop on the deck of the tiller flat, I can't imagine what Chatterton was bellyaching about.'

He made no reference to the smashed aircraft in the

hangar. With a glance at the navigator, Warren said. 'The matter of my being in arrest, sir. Do I take it – '

'Oh, just get out of my sight, Commander, do.'

'Aye, aye, sir.' Warren saluted and left the bridge. He went first to the tiller flat. Mason-Goodson had been, in fact, right: the hands were coping with the inflow of water, but the very presence of the water must indicate another seam sprung somewhere aft. This, the senior engineer officer said, was being looked for by the chief shipwright. And the steering engine was in full working order. Warren listened to the clatter of it as the quartermaster in the wheelhouse moved the helm to keep the ship's head driving into the wind and sea.

Mason-Goodson stared at the duffel-coated figure that had appeared on the bridge. 'Who are you and what do you want? Take that hood away from your face, man. It's obscuring you.'

'Yessir.' The hood of the duffel-coat was removed from the man's head. 'Shipwright's party, sir, to check the stability of the bridge superstructure, sir.'

'Really? I see.' Mason-Goodson's voice was icy. 'By whose order, may I ask?'

'Commander, sir. 'E –'

'Get off my bridge.'

'Sir, I – '

'I said, *get off my bridge*. Obey my order instantly.'

'Yessir. Sorry, sir.' With a baffled glance at the grim face of the navigating officer, the man left the bridge. Anderson said, 'I believe you'll regret that, sir.'

'When I wish your opinion, navigator, I shall ask for it. Until I do, hold your tongue, d'you hear me?'

'I heard you, sir. But I'm not going to hold my tongue when you're putting lives at risk – including your own. I believe the bridge to be unsafe, and – '

'Then you may save your own skin and get below. I shall not put up with insubordination. You may consider yourself relieved of your duties, and in arrest.'

'I shall not, sir. I'm needed here. I consider you a danger to the ship, and I'm perfectly prepared to justify that to the Admiralty.' Anderson was shaking with anger and his face was set hard; he had no intention of leaving the ship in Mason-Goodson's hands alone. As an officer of the Reserve he didn't suffer the same restraints and constrictions as a career officer of the RN. When the war was over he would go back to his shipping company and resume his own career leading to his own command. Mason-Goodson couldn't interfere with that. Not so long as he stuck to his post at a time of what he believed to be extreme danger. Something of this appeared to penetrate Mason-Goodson's mind. He said no more but simply turned his back.

Anderson would not leave it there. He said, 'I'm sending for the shipwright again, sir. And this time he's staying until a full check has been made.'

Mason-Goodson's reaction took Anderson by surprise. He said, 'There's a conspiracy against me in this ship and a full report will be made immediately on arrival in Norfolk. Disobedience of orders . . . the Commander, the chief bosun's mate. Now you.' He pushed past the binnacle, past Anderson, and went down the ladder without another word. Anderson bent to speak down the voice-pipe to the wheel-house. 'Quartermaster?'

'Sir?'

'Send down to the chief shipwright. I want one of his chaps up here again immediately. And ask the Commander to come to the bridge as soon as possible. The matter's urgent. Very urgent.' He straightened. Again he felt the curious motion of the bridge superstructure as the ship went on rolling violently. A welded ship . . . In his experience ships had been held together by rivets, and they had been immensely strong. He didn't feel happy in an all-welded ship and maybe that was why he was anxious. When a rivet was sprung it didn't necessarily have to mean other rivets would follow. It was different with welding. He recalled the fairly recent fate of the first all-welded ship to come out from an

American shipbuilding yard. She had been proceeding down the west coast towards the Panama Canal when the bottom had fallen out of her. Just like that – dropped straight off, and she had gone down with all hands. Like a stone.

On his way to the bridge in answer to the navigator's message, Warren, accompanied by a watchkeeping officer of *Charger*'s own complement, sent his messenger to find Lieutenant-Commander Cameron. He would be obliged if Cameron would go below to the tiller flat and be handy should anything go badly wrong. No panic, he said, but he had none of his own executive officers to spare and there was something of a leakage, a seepage into the compartment.

Then he continued up the ladders to the bridge. Anderson gave him a full report of the contretemps with the Captain.

'Where is he now?' Warren asked. The bridge had an empty look without Mason-Goodson's bulk at the fore screen.

'I don't know,' Anderson answered. 'He just went below without any explanation.' He told Warren of the Captain's remark about there being a conspiracy against him. That, Warren found worrying.

'A case for the doctor?' he asked doubtfully.

Anderson shrugged. 'A little extreme, perhaps. But a word mightn't be a bad thing. With full medical discretion. No reason why not.'

'Was there anything about God, pilot?'

Anderson gave a brief grin. 'Not this time.'

'You sent for the shipwright, you said. Any joy?'

'He's down on the sponson now. Looking at the main supports and that. Not a happy job in this weather.'

'Life-lines?'

'I made a point of stressing life-lines, but I didn't really need to. The buffer's down there as well. One of the RNVRs too, Jenkins.'

The Commander nodded. 'We're going to look a couple of bloody fools if the report's negative, pilot.'

'Yes. But I don't believe it's going to be.'

In the tiller flat, Cameron made his number with the senior engineer. 'Don't mind me,' he said. 'I won't interfere.'

'Decent of you.' Lieutenant(E) Tapp was inclined to sniff at what he thought of as the Saturday afternoon sailors of the RNVR. 'So what might you be here, for, eh?'

'At the Commander's request,' Cameron said mildly, all too well aware that neither he nor any of his officers and men had any official standing in the ship. 'Assist if necessary, that's all.'

'Uh-huh. Ever seen a tiller flat before, have you?'

'Not aboard a carrier.' Cameron held onto his temper.

'Carrier with a merchant ship hull. I suppose you know that if the water reaches the steering engine and buggers it up, the ship can't steer?'

'I know that, yes. Except by the pulley-hauley, of course.'

Tapp made no response to that; he, as well as Cameron, knew that if the steering engine stopped the ship would fall off the wind and sea long before tackles could be rigged and human muscle applied to the rudder-head. Cameron was surprised the ship's commander hadn't already ordered the tackles to be attached in readiness. That wouldn't be the engineers' job. Remarking on this, he said he would ring through to the bridge to get a party of seamen down to rig the tackles and then stand by in the tiller flat.

Five minutes later he was joined by ten seaman ratings under a leading hand together with his own buffer-to-be, Petty Officer Berridge.

'Commander's orders, sir.' Berridge added, 'Ship's own buffer, sir, Chief PO Stoner, he's standing by the lash-up in the hangar, and the captains of the tops,' he said in reference to the divisional petty officers, 'they're clearing up damage in their own parts-of-ship. She's taking a fair old battering, sir, that she is.'

'What's it like in the hangar now, buff?'

'Bloody awful, sir. Never seen such a load of debris, and it shifts with every movement of the ship.' PO Berridge pushed his cap to the back of his head and mopped at his forehead with the back of a hand. 'Right, now, lads, let's get them tackles rigged and ready and hope to God we don't need to use them. Proper sod's job that'd be, worst possible way to steer a ship.'

He could say that again, Cameron thought. He'd done it himself, just once, in a destroyer, also in the North Atlantic. He'd hoped never to have to do it again.

As the hands worked, the water continued its seepage. It was deepening; not much, but any deepening was alarming. If the pumps were failing to cope already, the outlook if the leak should worsen was not a very happy one.

Mason-Goodson had gone to his cabin: not his seacabin but his normal harbour quarters, consisting of a large day cabin, sitting room and dining room combined, and a sleeping cabin with private shower and lavatory. In the day cabin was a roll-top desk such as was supplied for the use of all Post Captains in the British fleet. Originally Mason-Goodson had found he was expected to make do with a US-type desk, an affair largely of steel with a fake leather writing surface. He had made a fuss about this, representing his annoyance to the British Naval Liaison Officer attached to the Embassy in Washington when he had arrived in Portland, Oregon, to commission the ship and take her over from the Willamette yard. When a few weeks later he had brought his brand-new command into the Firth of Clyde to begin operations of war, the proper Admiralty pattern desk had been awaiting him and had been duly embarked and fitted in place.

Not without trouble.

There had been a trade union dispute which Mason-Goodson had found distasteful. It appeared that the civilian shipyard carpenters had regarded the transport and placing of the desk to be a shipyard job and because of sickness (which Mason-Goodson had called skrimshanking) and holidays (quite unnecessary in wartime) the job could not be done at once. A three-day delay had been spoken of. Mason-Goodson, furious at such obstructive tactics, had said this was poppycock, and had sent a party of seamen ashore in the ship's own motor cutter. With the after canopy stripped away, the desk had been loaded into the sternsheets and brought back to the ship, where it had been hoisted to the flight deck by the carrier's own aircraft derrick and thence manhandled down to the Captain's quarters. All done by his own ship's company and the devil take the trade unionists and all other socialists.

The result had been a strike of carpenters in the yards all the way down the Clyde from the Broomielaw in Glasgow to the Tail o' the Bank. The Flag Officer in Charge had become embroiled and Mason-Goodson had been required to state his reasons for his actions. As a result he had been faced with an unpleasant interview with FOIC. He had, he was told, interfered seriously with the refitting of vital ships. He had been required to make an apology to the shore carpenters' shop steward.

This episode had left Mason-Goodson with a seething hatred of trade unions. And now, out at sea of all places, he was being faced with a somewhat similar situation. Officers of the Royal Naval Reserve were all basically Merchant Service officers and they had a trade union – whatever else they cared to call it. The Officers' Federation, which included the Navigating and Engineer Officers' Union, was just that: a trade union.

That man Anderson.

It was so typical. Rude, arrogant, self-opinionated. A good seaman certainly, a knowledgeable and competent navigator. No doubt those Clydesdale carpenters had also been good at their job. Good tradesmen. All trade unionists.

Mason-Goodson sat down at his roll-top desk and opened it with a key from a ring attached to a lanyard around his waist beneath his uniform jacket. He began writing a report on Anderson that would shortly be typed by his secretary, a paymaster sub-lieutenant, and forwarded to the Admiralty on arrival in Norfolk Navy Yard. Writing was currently not easy; the carrier was rolling very badly and there was a constant racket from the wind and straining metal and the drumming from the hangar deck below where the debris was still on the move, sliding from side to side and back again on the roll. The constant noise cut into Mason-Goodson's thoughts. And it was difficult to stop himself falling sideways. Also to keep control of the bottle of ink when he found he had to refill his fountain-pen. The bottle in fact took charge, sliding from the desk onto the carpet, where blue-black spread in a circle before running hither and thither on the roll and pitch of the ship.

Mason-Goodson was about to ring for his steward when an alarming noise came from somewhere on the starboard side of the ship.

It was a noise of foreboding, a noise of metal reaching breaking point. Never mind the ink now: Mason-Goodson left his cabin at the rush, going out onto the walkway where Nelson the cat had been spotted just prior to his escape to the flight deck.

When it happened, it happened very suddenly: precisely what Anderson had feared. There had been a yell from the starboard for'ard sponson below the bridge superstructure and as Anderson went to the side and looked over two bodies were seen to hurtle down into the sea and then disappear somewhere beneath the ship. In the same instant there was a tearing sound followed by a kind of grinding and Anderson lurched half over the guard rail. Before anyone on the bridge or in the wheel-house immediately below could react, the whole superstructure – bridge, flying control, wheelhouse – tore away from the ship together with the ladders and sea-cabin and the access hatches. It all hung for a brief moment as though reluctant to part company, then it went over with a kind of shriek of finally ripping metal, fell away and vanished beneath the waves, banging and clanging along the skin of the double bottoms for a moment before plunging into the depths.

With it went the human cargo: Commander, navigator, Officer of the Watch and the lieutenant who had accompanied Warren to the bridge earlier . . . the yeoman of the watch, bosun's mate, bridge messenger, port and starboard lookouts, together with the quartermaster and telegraphsmen from the compartment that had been the wheelhouse.

Within the next minute the ship, no longer under steerage, had fallen off the wind and sea and lay helpless in the trough between two eight-foot waves, wallowing broadside on to the full force of nature on the warpath.

Mason-Goodson, who had reached the ladder to the bridge in the very moment that overstrained metal had at last given way, had been catapulted backwards, thrown clear of the ladder and the gaping hold left by the parting of the superstructure. Semi-conscious, he lay wrapped around a stanchion of the walkway leading from his quarters, dangling in a dazed heap over the hangar deck below.

6

THERE WAS confusion bordering on pande-
monium throughout the ship now. Aware of something
drastic having happened, the chief engineer tried to make
contact with the bridge, failing because it was no longer there.
All over the engine spaces – engine-room, boiler-room with
the oil-fed furnaces – men slithered helplessly as the decks
went haywire. Some of the stokers were flung bodily against
the boiler plates and there were many burns from the flaring,
white-hot innards of the furnaces. In other parts of the ship
there was total chaos, everything that had not been made fast
flying around: stores, offices, galleys, pantries, wardroom
and messdecks. Mess traps, bread barges, spitkids . . . bottles
of gin and whisky, vast butts of cocoa simmering away in the
galley spilled their contents, sides of beef took charge in the
butcher's stores, in the surgery the operating table went for a
burton amid a welter of tablets and broken glass. . . .

In the tiller flat the steering engine went dead: it had
succumbed to the rising water. Already they had seen that the
ship was no longer steering from the wheelhouse. To
Cameron it was obvious that they had broached to. The
moment the falling-off of the ship's head had been observed
on the gyro repeater, which had spun round, clicking madly,
Cameron had sent the seamen to man the tackles on the
rudder-head, tackles whose other ends were secured to heavy
ringbolts set into the deck of the tiller flat. The theory was that

the ship could in emergency be steered by hauling on the crossbar on the rudder-head, hauling on one side and walking back on the other so that the rudder was turned. In emergency. It was the worst sort of emergency now.

The gyro repeater showed that the ship's head was now due south. As in the case of the chief engineer, there was no response when Cameron tried to contact the bridge. In what appeared to be the absence of command, he took charge himself.

'We have to get her back on a westerly course,' he said to Berridge. 'Head into wind and sea – and fast.'

'Tall order, sir, but I reckon we'll beat the bugger.' Berridge passed the order to the hands on the tackles. 'Leave the port tackle,' he said. 'All hands, back up starboard. With a will now, lads. You're our best hope.' The only one, he thought to himself, seeing as the steering engine had packed up. '*Heave away, all your weight now!*' He mucked in with the rest. So did Cameron and Tapp. With sweat and laboured breathing and a number of oaths, the rudder-head came round.

The ship did not.

Cameron had sent a hand to contact the bridge and report back. When the man returned, looking white and scared, and made his report of no bridge superstructure but a gaping hole in the flight deck, Cameron left the tiller flat in the charge of PO Berridge and went up topsides.

Water was coming down in intermittent cascades as the ship floundered in the trough, sogged, unworkable, a dead thing as it seemed even though the main engine, still obeying the last order, was moving at full ahead. In the hangar, staring up at the hole above, Cameron found the chief shipwright looking shaken to the core. Half his party had gone over the side, he said.

'Can you do anything about that hole?' Cameron asked.

'We can always try the bloody impossible, sir.'

'I suggest you give it a go, then. What happened to the ship's officers, d'you know?'

The chief shipwright told him: Commander, navigator, all the bridge personnel. There seemed to be no one in charge, what with the officers lost earlier. Then Cameron became aware of the humped figure on the walkway, bunched against a stanchion but shifting dangerously as the ship lurched to the weight of the water dropping down onto her flight deck.

'Looks like the Captain, chief. Give me a hand.'

They plunged through the water that was deepening on the hangar deck, making for the port-side ladder leading to the walkway where Mason-Goodson lay unconscious. There was a deep gash on the Captain's forehead and his legs lay at awkward angles; but there was a heartbeat. 'We'll get him to his cabin,' Cameron said. 'After that – we'll see.'

The situation was as bad as it possibly could be. Total loss of the ship seemed inevitable. No assistance could be expected from the escorting destroyers who were facing their own difficulties. No boats could be got away from any of the ships in the prevailing conditions. The destroyers had been signalling by light whenever they could train their lamps on the wallowing carrier but there had been no response. So far as Cameron could make out, all the ship's executive officers with the exception of the Captain himself had now been lost: and Mason-Goodson was in no fit state to exercise command. The PMO had reported a deep wound to the head and both ankles broken. And Mason-Goodson was currently still unconscious.

Cameron was in a dilemma. Someone had to take command. He was aware of the naval regulations concerning the chain of command. In the event of action casualties, the next senior officer of the executive branch took over. If all the executive officers were lost, then command devolved on the senior rating of the seaman branch, in the current case Chief Petty Officer Stoner.

In the hangar after leaving the Captain in his cabin, Cameron found a muster of the hands, a muster called by Stoner himself, of all seamen and miscellaneous ratings except those at the pumps and in the tiller flat, the engine-room complement remaining at their posts below.

Stoner confirmed that all the executive officers were lost.

'You know what that means, chief,' Cameron said.

'Yessir. By the regulations, sir. But there's you.'

'I'm only a passenger. I've no authority.'

'In the circumstances, sir. With respect, sir. You've a duty to take over.' Stoner grinned tightly. 'Me, I don't reckon I'd like to take over this little lot.'

Cameron nodded. Then he raised his voice to speak to the mustered seamen. 'I'm taking over the command in an acting capacity until the Captain's fit for duty. Lieutenant Grey will act as first lieutenant. Now we all have to save the ship, and normal watches will be suspended until we have. There are two priorities at this moment: to plug the hole in the flight deck before the ship floods, and to get her head back into the wind and sea. And thank God the engine-room's still functioning.'

Because the engine-room was still functioning they not only had power on the main engine but they also had power, and therefore light, throughout the ship. Apart from the super-structure the only casualty, and that a potentially lethal one, was the succumbing of the steering engine to the rising water in the tiller flat. The pumps were now going at full blast and if the water could be got out of the tiller flat, so Chatterton said, then the steering engine would be overhauled and brought back into commission. But this was not going to happen until the inrush of water to the hangar was brought under control by plugging the gap in the flight deck and sealing the opened-up welded seam in the hangar side, a ferociously difficult task with the hull laid over at an angle by the sea's action.

Cameron spoke to Neil Grey. 'What do you make the chances, Number One?'

Grey shrugged. 'Not much to be done about the weld. The shipwright ought to be able to keep the water out of that hole, anyway to a large extent. Planks, tarpaulins. It's the steering that's the worst thing. We can't last all that long unless we can get out of the trough.'

'Which really means that keeping back the water is the first thing, get the steering engine working again. Better have all possible hands to back up the shipwrights. Except the party in the tiller flat.'

Cameron went below again to the tiller flat. The seamen looked ready to drop as they hauled on the tackle. Cameron saw that currently theirs was a hopeless task and he told PO Berridge to leave it and use the hands to deal with the floodwater. If only the wind would drop, even just a little, they might be able to bring her round . . . or again they might not. A gale of the current weight was going to leave pretty mountainous seas behind it for quite a while after it had blown itself right out.

One of the scary things about lying broached-to was the comparative silence. The wind was cut off, very largely, deflected by the great crests above, so it was heard more or less distantly. The normal engine sounds of a ship at sea were now absent as well; in conference with the lieutenant-commander(E) Cameron had suggested there was little point in keeping the engine moving.

'While we can't steer,' he said. 'It's not doing any good.'

Chatterton agreed. 'Not only that. There's the question of bunkers. I'm bunkered for a straight run to Norfolk. If this goes on we could run short.'

'Stop engines, then, chief.'

The engine died, the great shaft ceasing its spin. There was more than a slop of water on the engine-room deck by this time. It seemed the pumps were not quite coping. With Chatterton, when the engine-room stood in an uneasy stillness, Cameron went down the hatch to have a look at the double bottoms, squeezing behind a torch through the narrow apertures in the transverse bulkheads amid a stifling stench of stale air, oil and the general muck that included the rotting corpses of rats, mice and cockroaches. And water. It was an unpleasant experience, to be so confined in the very bottom of a badly canted ship, separated only by a hair's breadth from the raging sea.

They came up thankfully. 'Not good,' Chatterton commented in reference to the water. 'Not good for stability when we're laid over like we are.'

'What can we do about it?' Cameron asked.

Chatterton gave a hard laugh. 'Apart from the pumps – bugger all!'

The ship went on wallowing. The situation was on a knife-edge. Shifted gear throughout the carrier was adding to the forces that were giving her the heavy list. Everything that had not been secured had slid over to port. The port side of the hangar deck was filled with the debris from the shattered aircraft, which lay piled up in heaps against the port bulkhead. By now all hands not working at the pumps or in the tiller flat had been cleared from the lower deck: Cameron had spoken again to the ship's company, telling them the situation without holding back. The ship, he said, might go at any moment. Relief watches were organized by the buffer, Chief PO Stoner, with Malting's assistance in regard to the draft for the *Veracity* in the distant Norfolk Navy Yard. These reliefs, working in two-hour shifts, would keep the pumps and tiller flat manned. The PO Cook and his galley staff would be allowed below to rustle up what food and drink could be provided, iron rations to keep the hands going. Some success had been achieved by the shipwrights' party in plugging the hole in the flight deck: a bird's-nest of planks and tarpaulins was doing its job, though it was far from completely watertight and seawater was trickling through to drop onto the men hanging on where they could in the hangar, cold, wet through, miserable. And scared.

Somebody was doing something to combat the cold. The ship's master-at-arms, MAA Horner, was seen coming up from below with his regulating petty officer and two leading hands. Between them they carried barricoes of navy rum, the daily issue of grog for the hands.

MAA Horner approached Cameron and saluted.

'Rum, sir. Up spirits, like. Just in case you wanted to splice the mainbrace, sir.'

Cameron said, 'Why not? They've earned it.'

'Just what I thought, sir. Permission to carry on, sir?'

Cameron nodded. 'No cups, I suppose?'

'They'll not be worrying about that, sir.' The master-at-arms and his party made the issue, the men lining up and taking the rum straight from the polished copper dipper. The rum had not been diluted with three parts of water as was the regulation issue for leading hands and below: today, they were getting it neat. Cameron wondered briefly how the paymaster was going to square that with his records. A similar thought seemed to have occurred to Ben Malting, who was standing alongside Cameron.

'A pound to a penny the Admiralty'll raise a stink, sir.'

'You're probably right, buff.'

'Mean set o' bastards, I reckon, sir, all done by the book.' Ben Malting had been ashore on night leave from Pompey barracks when Goering's *Luftwaffe* had dropped a land mine on the petty officers' mess, back in the spring of '41. There hadn't been enough warning to get all the POs out of the block and into the air raid shelters beneath the parade ground; numbers of them had been blown into little pieces. The next night, in Ben's Queen Street pub, he and Bessie had pulled as many pints on the house as could be drunk by the survivors, and never mind that the pub had had all its windows blown out and a chimney down through a spare bedroom. The Admiralty wouldn't have behaved like that.

When the mainbrace had been spliced satisfactorily – the splicing of the mainbrace being the Navy's euphemism for an extra rum issue – Cameron climbed to the starboard for'ard walkway. There was not very much point in keeping a watch aboard a ship that lay totally helpless, but nevertheless an officer of the *Veracity*'s draft had been positioned at the for'ard end of the walkway to keep a watch in two-hour shifts like the hands. This was for form's sake: the ship's company would expect an officer to be on the alert and watching out.

Cameron clambered out onto the steel framework: much of it had been torn away when the superstructure went, was a tangle of twisted metal with its end dangling down over the sea. One of Cameron's sub-lieutenants was currently on watch, hanging on, as it seemed, for his life.

Cameron grinned at him. 'Scared, sub?'

'Not really, sir.'

'Come off it – we all are. Nothing to be ashamed of. Just so long as you don't let it all get you down. I – ' He broke off as a massive wave curled to its full height and began to drop, its crest turning over in white foam. 'Hang on,' he shouted. They both clung fast to what was left of the guardrail as the wave dropped, crashing down on their bodies, thumping them into the bottom plating of the walkway before draining away through the open metalwork and across the flight deck so sharply canted over to port. Then, rolling away beneath, the residue of the wave lifted the ship bodily before dropping her back like a dead whale into the trough.

The sub-lieutenant was white-faced, shivering with the appalling cold and wet. And with fear, Cameron knew. But he was fighting through. He met Cameron's eye. 'Nasty one, sir. Not the first.'

'I know that, sub. Just think about the old-timers, the shellbacks fighting their way round Cape Horn under square sail. They survived.'

'It couldn't have been worse than this,' the sub said.

'No, probably not. But when we come through – and we will, never doubt that – well, you'll be a seaman. Just like they were.'

Cameron made his way below again, ducking under the overhang of the flight deck. He was thinking: what use is it going to be to that lad, to be a seaman, when this war's over? Sub-lieutenant Read was RNVR, in civilian life an accounts clerk working in a London store – Piccadilly, where the only dangers in peacetime were the busy nightly attentions of the street walkers. He probably wasn't even there at night: he'd lived with his parents in Pinner, right out in the country. Why should he wish to be a seaman? Nevertheless, it was the best praise Cameron knew.

It was never-ending. The pumps worked flat out and somehow they kept the ship afloat. In that lay their hope: if she hadn't gone yet, maybe she wouldn't go at all. Maybe she'd come through the worst. Maybe she'd survive until the gale had blown itself out and then – well, they'd see. See what was to be done. With better weather, and the destroyer escort still in contact, they could be transferred by the seaboats to safety. And leave the ship to wallow – in which case she would become a floating danger to the convoys crossing to and from American ports. Maybe they would have to open the seacocks and let her drown, go down into the bitter depths of the North Atlantic.

Cameron was about to go down to give some encouragement to the men in the tiller flat when a high shout came from the walkway above, a yell of near hysteria that ran around the hangar, a warning as it seemed to be, a garbled one.

Scrabbling along the sloping deck, spider-like, Cameron made with all possible speed for the ladder and climbed fast. Reaching the open walkway he gave a gasp. Only just ahead of the wallowing carrier's bows, clear by little more than a couple of cables'-lengths, an enormous shape was poised across two of the rearing wave crests, a great hull in camouflage paint that seemed to blot out the sky, a hull topped by three gigantic funnels.

The sub was looking green. As well he might. Wallowing in the troughs, the carrier would have been obscured by the waves from the other ship's radar, probably obscured from sight too by those waves and the appalling visibility. As the great vessel moved away beyond the crests Cameron spoke.

'Close shave,' he said.

'Yes. . . .'

'But all's well now, sub. Something to tell your grandchildren about one day! That was the *Queen Mary* . . . bound for the Clyde, very likely with a whole American division embarked.'

A very close shave. But if by some stroke of luck they had been spotted from the *Queen Mary*'s bridge, then a report would be made on the liner's arrival at the Tail o' the Bank. Though what anyone could do about them was, to say the least, problematic.

7

As THE next dark came down, they huddled on the hangar deck, close together to share the warmth of their bodies. Some while earlier Cameron had ordered the evacuation of the tiller flat, also the engine-room and boiler-room: the engines were not going to be required in current circumstances and men couldn't be left below unnecessarily with the possibility that the ship might go at any moment; though in all truth they would be no better off in the hangar if the end should come – which was the point made by Chatterton.

'Nobody's going to be able to abandon and have any hope of coming through – are they? And we'll be warmer down below.'

Cameron wouldn't have it. There was always a chance – little enough admittedly – that some of the hands might be picked up by the escort if they managed to scramble clear of the hangar in time. But from the engine spaces there would be no hope at all. The same consideration applied to the men in the tiller flat. So now they were all together in the hangar, some 450 men. Just waiting. There was nothing more anyone could do.

Cameron got them singing: singing always helped. Some rousing choruses, seamen's songs. Mostly filthy, but there were no women around to hear, and the noise, echoing round the hangar, overlaid the formidable sound of the pounding sea.

Inside themselves they were all reacting in their different ways. Some were obviously dead scared, others were phlegmatic. What was to come would come and they would have no say in it; and throughout the years of war at sea death had always been close even though you didn't spend too much of your time thinking about it. A good many now thought about God, some of them for the first time in any really serious way.

Mason-Goodson had partially recovered consciousness, was aware that he was in his cabin and in pain, attended by his steward, Lawson, and a sick-berth attendant. He was aware that he was unable to move his legs, which had been put in plaster by the doctor. Also, he was strapped down in his bunk against the sharp cant of the ship.

He asked for the Commander.

'Lost, sir,' Lawson told him. 'Lost overboard, sir.' The steward went on to tell him what had happened. Told him that the navigator had gone as well, and all the others who had been on the bridge and in the wheelhouse.

'I'll be damned,' Mason-Goodson said. He said no more, but he remembered what Anderson had said so insistently. He had never imagined for one moment that it would happen. But Anderson had been right after all, apparently. That boat they'd sighted . . . that strong impulse he'd had, sent to him by God. Why had not God seen to it that good, not evil, had followed his answer to the call? Mason-Goodson asked for a Bible. The answer might be there, perhaps.

'A Bible, sir?'

'That's what I said. Get it.'

There had never, to the steward's knowledge, been a Bible in the Captain's quarters. This God business was something new. He rememembered hearing yarns along the messdeck, how the skipper had chased the buffer about the lack of a Bible in the seaboat's equipment.

'No Bible here, sir.'

'Find one. At once. And get the doctor.'

'Yessir.'

Lawson left the cabin, left the Captain in the care of the SBA. This was a fine time to go in search of a Bible. Wasn't as though they had a padre aboard, a Holy Joe who'd be bound to have a Bible. Lawson found the surgeon lieutenant sitting close to the paymaster lieutenant-commander. He reported the Captain's condition. And his wish.

'Is he fully conscious, Lawson?'

'Yessir.'

'Wandering?'

'I don't think so, sir, no. Asked about the Commander an' that.'

'I'll come up,' the surgeon lieutenant said. 'But I haven't got a Bible. . . .'

When with difficulty he reached the Captain's bedside, Mason-Goodson was alseep. He woke, however, when the doctor gently lifted one of his eyelids. 'Who's that?' he asked.

'Surgeon lieutenant, sir. I'm sorry to say I haven't – '

'Who is looking after my ship?'

'The officer in charge of the draft for – '

'Cameron, do you mean?'

'Yes, sir.'

Mason-Goodson tried to lift the top half of his body. He failed, dropped back with an expression of pain. 'God damn,' he said. 'I'm not having that. *I am not having that*, d'you hear me? Get Cameron here at once.'

Mr Trimby, warrant engineer, chief engineer-to-be of the *Veracity*, was another who was thinking about God, though in a way different from Mason-Goodson. His thoughts were not questioning but fearful.

Adultery was, of course, a sin. No two ways about that, and death might be very close. He was very likely going to have to face up to things past at any moment. God would not be pleased and would side with Maud, bound to. And one day Maud would also be going aloft, as would her sister.

When that happened, all hell, though Mr Trimby did try not to think of that word, would be let loose.

What could he do about it?

Sod all.

Mr Trimby shook. It wasn't the bitter cold and his wet clothing. It was sheer naked funk. He could see it all quite clearly, the angry God, the Ultimate Judge as his old mother used to call Him, pronouncing sentence. The terrible fires of hell with their attendant demons and torturers armed with long spiked poles to push you into the blazing ovens that never, in actual fact, burned you right through, so that you continued suffering for ever, life everlasting. It wasn't fair, not really, too bloody much altogether as retribution for a simple fuck. Maybe, after all, God would understand – he certainly would when eventually he came up against Maud. Then he might relent, and Mr Trimby would be withdrawn from the ovens, from the devil's horrible kingdom. Prince of Darkness they called the devil, according to his old mother who'd been very religious. A pity he hadn't listened to his old mother all those years ago when she'd gone on about sin and the Garden of Eden and the whatsit, apple.

Mr Trimby gave a loud sigh.

The *Veracity*'s gunner, Mr Fielder, was hunched alongside him. 'You all right?' he asked. 'Not that any of us are.'

'I'm all right.' Having spoken, Mr Trimby had a sudden thought. They said, whoever 'they' might be, that it helped to talk about things, get them out of your system, get some sort of reassurance. Then things didn't look so black. The gunner, a man of his own rank and probably, though Mr Trimby had not met him previously, of a similar experience – going ashore, boozing, all that sort of thing, the normal naval life – Fielder would be likely to understand his dilemma, his fears for what might be the immediate future, the future that could conceivably come with the next wave passing beneath the double bottoms.

Worth a try. Nothing venture, Mr Trimby thought, nothing gained. His old mother had never said that, but Mr Trimby had once been a boy scout.

He nudged Mr Fielder. 'What you just said, Guns.'

'What about?'

'Was I all right. I'm not. Bloody far from it.'

'Sorry to hear that, Mr Trimby. Mean I can help?'

'Maybe, yes.' It wasn't easy, but Mr Trimby explained, or tried to, starting off with a reference to God and their current predicament. 'Fear of death,' he said bluntly in the end, because Mr Fielder didn't seem to be cottoning on.

'No use worrying about the inevitable, Mr Trimby. We all got to go some time. Soon or late, makes no difference, not really.'

'No. I see that. But there's some things . . . well, things you don't want to face up to like. If you get my meaning. Things you didn't ought to have done. Things God'll get at you for.' Mr Trimby was approaching his point. 'To do with the ladies, like,' he said with an effort.

'Ah. It's that way, is it?'

'Yes.'

'Doing what you didn't ought.'

'Yes.'

'Well,' the gunner said judicially, rather flattered at being appealed to, his advice sought. 'It all depends, don't it? Maybe God looks at things in different ways. Different people, see. Depends on the circumstances. I reckon – '

Mr Trimby blurted it out suddenly. 'I got caught out.'

'Ah. In the . . . er . . . act?'

Mr Trimby nodded.

'*That* don't make any difference. Not to God it don't.' Mr Fielder frowned in thought, dredged up some relevant panaceas from the past. 'My old mother, she – '

'You got an old mother too, eh?'

'We most of us do,' the gunner said, giving Mr Trimby a sardonic sideways look. 'Not now. She passed on. She was never worried about death. What she said was, God's mercy is infinite. See? You'd best keep that in mind. So long as you repent.'

'Apologize like?'

'Well – pray.'

Mr Trimby thought it might be rather late now, praying only when he was right up against it. God, if he was at all like any skipper RN, would see through that one in very quick time. He risked a question. 'You ever – you know?'

'Yes,' Mr Fielder said. 'Course I have.'

'Never got caught out?'

'No.'

Quite where that got him, Mr Trimby didn't really know, but it was comforting in its way. The gunner evidently wasn't worried about the future. Mr Trimby had an emerging feeling, or anyway a hope, that he himself wouldn't have been so worried if he hadn't been caught out that day by Maud. It was the memory of that that nagged.

Like Mr Trimby, Ben Malting's thoughts were where so many of the ship's company's thoughts were turning: home, with wives or parents. Malting wasn't much worried about Bessie, who was a very capable woman who would just carry on running the pub, even without his advice behind her. Of course, she would miss him; they'd always been very close. But that was a different consideration; Malting was a practical man, and his main consideration would be not to leave his widow without financial support and that didn't apply to Bessie. Not currently, anyway. What did worry him as the ship lay so heavily in the wave troughs and the booming sound of the seas impacting on her exposed starboard plates came like the knell of doom, was Marianne and her carryings on. With no father in the background God alone knew what she'd get up to. Get herself pregnant sooner or later; before long she would be bound to let some unsavoury youth go too far, get past her guard.

And scandal of that sort didn't help a publican's reputation with the licensing justices. Or with the brewery. Especially in the case of a widow licensee. There could be all sorts of bother.

Bessie was going to have her work cut out in regard to Marianne and that was a nasty, nagging thought at a time like this. Marianne was incorrigible, always had been. Ben Malting's thoughts went back to when Marianne was five. He'd been on leave, just home from a commission in the Med, two years away. In the interval Marianne had grown from a three-year-old romping baby into a very, very precocious child. They'd been asked round to a birthday party at the home of a petty officer from Ben's last ship. It was the PO's six-year-old kid that was having the birthday and it was Marrianne who'd wrecked it. She had been discovered in the outside privy at the bottom of a long, narrow garden, one of many long, narrow gardens side by side in a road off Arundel Street in Portsea, letting her knickers down for a penny a look. Ben's PO friend had made light of it, laughing it off good-naturedly, and commenting that it showed a useful commercial streak, a comment that could be taken two ways and had infuriated Bessie, thus causing the end of a friendship.

Marianne hadn't repeated that performance. Not so far as Ben knew.

Cameron answered the summons to the Captain's sleeping cabin. He found the PMO there: Surgeon Lieutenant-Commander MacAllister. MacAllister said Mason-Goodson was sleeping and was not to be disturbed.

'He's relapsed,' he said briefly. 'He wasn't fully conscious when I came up. There's some amnesia. He's not accepting that the bridge has gone, or the Commander and the rest. I gather from his steward that he took it in at first but now it's gone.'

'So what do we do?' Cameron asked.

MacAllister shrugged. 'Wait and see. There's no treatment. The ankles will mend. Obviously, the blow to his head has caused the amnesia, but the actual physical wound is healing satisfactorily. There's nothing else I can do except keep him warm.'

'His life's not in danger, PMO?'

MacAllister laughed. 'No more than the rest of us, no. If we

81

make the Norfolk base, he'll be with us and can be landed for a full investigation.'

Later that day, as the carrier's list increased slightly, it was decided to shift Mason-Goodson from his quarters. The sharply canted angle of his bunk was not helping, and the journeys to and from his cabin along the walkway beneath the flight deck were becoming too hazardous. There was also the question of getting Mason-Goodson clear if the end should be seen to be approaching. In the hangar he would have whatever chance was going, the same chance as anyone else aboard. Isolated at the end of the walkway he wouldn't have a hope. So he was strapped, heavily blanketed, into a Neil Robertson stretcher and lowered by a tackle rigged by Chief PO Stoner into the hangar where the stretcher was secured to a ringbolt in the deck.

Chief PO Stoner had his problems, family ones, though not concerned with wives and errant offspring. Stoner, a big-built man with a jaw like a rock, a stern disciplinarian who would in fact have liked nothing more than to have brought up a clean-living, God-fearing brood of children, had never married. Often tempted, he had resisted. He had resisted because he had a self-imposed duty to his two parents, now approaching their middle eighties. Shortly after he had joined the navy as a seaman boy in the old training ship, or stone frigate, HMS *St Vincent* at Gosport across the harbour from Portsmouth, his mother had been struck down by a stroke and had been helpless ever since. Soon after that his father had suffered an accident during his employment as a shipwright in the dockyard. As the result of this accident he had lost both his legs and had been paralysed down one side. He had of course been unable to work since then and although there was some compensation from the industrial injuries people, Stoner's parents had been virtually unable to exist. There had at first been some assistance from charities, and Stoner's two uncles had also helped so far as they were able on their wages. Then one uncle had died; and after being rated able seaman, young Stoner had assumed the responsibility for his parents, allotting almost the whole of his two shillings a day pay for their support. He didn't smoke; he didn't drink, not even the daily tot of rum, for which he drew in lieu the sum of threepence a day. It all helped mum and dad.

That support had continued throughout his career: good-conduct badges, three eventually, meant extra pay, as did advancement in rank and in his non-substantive rating. Leading Seaman, Petty Officer, Chief Petty Officer . . . seaman gunner, captain of the gun first-class, gunlayer.

He'd done well; but with mum and dad to support, he couldn't even think about marriage.

Now he had plenty to think about. If the ship went, how ever would his parents manage? Stoner himself had a life assurance policy but a far from big one, might keep them for a year or so. With the war, money had begun to lose its value and God knew where that process was going to end. And, again if he went in the next few hours or sooner, there would be no compensation paid to parents and no pension to anyone other than a wife. And he was the last of the family: the other uncle had been killed in one of the early air raids over Pompey and Stoner himself had no brothers or sisters.

That Cameron, now.

He carried a load of responsibility that he didn't even know about. Not just the ship itself, not just the men. Indirectly he carried the lives of Stoner's old mum and dad, and loads of other family concerns as well. Had some of his own too, likely enough. No one was really on his own in this world.

Stoner, as he supervised the securing of the Captain's stretcher to the ringbolt, reflected that it was possible someone even loved Mason-Goodson, doubtful as that proposition might seem to any of his ship's company. Proper old bastard, was the skipper . . . but he had a wife, Stoner knew that, having seen her once when she'd come aboard at the Tail o' the Bank. She'd looked nice, quite a few years younger than Mason-Goodson, had a nice smile and, according to the Captain's steward, a friendly way with her, not stuffy like many skippers' wives. The skipper, when he'd seen her over the side to go back to wherever she was staying in Greenock or more likely Gourock, had been pretty off-hand. He had been heard to say to the Commander after she'd gone off in the motor-cutter – Stoner had happened to be within earshot – that normally he never allowed his wife to come within twenty miles of any port he'd entered.

But maybe she loved him.

From time to time Mason-Goodson came through the mists, but never for very long. He rambled mostly, muttering something about a lack of Bibles. He spoke also of knowing that there was a conspiracy against him. The ringleader was the Commander. At one point he asked quite clearly for the Commander to report to him immediately.

It was Neil Grey who answered. 'The Commander's – ' He broke off: the Captain wasn't taking things in but there was nothing to be gained by possibly exacerbating his mental condition. Grey changed what he'd been going to say. 'I'll see that he's informed, sir.'

The next moment Mason-Goodson relapsed into unconsciousness again. When next he came round briefly he seemed to have forgotten about the Commander. There was a lot of confused muttering about the boatload that had been sighted earlier, and about the visible hand of God.

'A direct message,' he said.

'Yes, sir.'

'I was selected, you see.' For a moment he seemed to rally further, staring at Grey with his eyes focussing. 'Who the devil are you, may I ask?'

Grey said who he was.

'You understand, perhaps. You realize that I was chosen.'

'Yes, sir.'

'Not many do. There are so many unbelievers.'

'I dare say there are, sir.'

'But not you. I can see that.'

'Yes, sir.'

'Stay by me,' Mason-Goodson said. 'By my side. Don't leave me. I need your support.'

Grey looked round, caught Cameron's eye. Cameron gave a nod. Grey said, 'Of course, sir, I'll do that.'

'It's an order, Mr Christian.'

'Christ – ' Grey broke off, stared across Mason-Goodson towards Cameron again. Mason-Goodson's head fell sideways and his eyes closed. He began breathing heavily: unconscious again. 'Mr Christian,' Grey repeated incredulously. 'Captain Bligh, Bligh of the *Bounty*. I wonder what that meant?'

The PMO was close by. He said, 'Some sort of . . . thought transference perhaps.'

'You mean he thinks he's Captain Bligh? Bligh, facing a mutiny, two hundred and whatever years ago?'

The PMO shrugged. 'It sounds fairly possible, doesn't it, taking into account what he's been saying about a conspiracy against him. We really don't know much – if anything – about the mind and its processes. The trick-cyclists think they do. I'm just a country GP in disguise.' MacAllister was RNVR, had had a practice in the north of Scotland, covering a wide area. He'd not had much experience of mental matters; the Scots, he often said, kept that sort of thing at bay with whisky, very sensibly. He went on, 'Perhaps he was Bligh in a previous existence, who knows?'

No one did. It could all link up with Mason-Goodson's newly acquired intimacy with the Almighty, who'd chosen him to find those survivors.

The word spread through the hangar: the skipper was having hallucinations, believed himself to be Captain Bligh. Prewar, there had been a film about Bligh of the *Bounty* and quite a few had seen it, those who'd been regular RN having a vested interest in domineering captains. Bligh had been a right sod, flogging men and keel-hauling them, all manner of cruelties that had led his First Lieutenant, Mr Christian, to lead a mutiny against him. The men aboard the

Charger reckoned it was fortunate the skipper was imprisoned in a Neil Robertson stretcher, which in essence was like a straitjacket.

The PMO, it was stated as a fact by the time the buzz had reached the most-distant part of the hangar, had said the skipper had probably been Captain Bligh in a previous existence. That might or might not be the case; it depended on your individual belief. But it was always a possibility and doctors didn't shoot their mouths off without knowing what they were talking about. A sour-faced able seaman elaborated, giving a sneering laugh. 'If the skipper *was* Bligh last time round, or the time before more likely, that might explain the God angle – eh? Bin up in front of Him before, defaulter, under escort o' St Paul acting Master-at-Arms.' The AB assumed a hectoring, master-at-arms-like tone. 'Double march . . . 'alt. Orf cap. Salute the Lord. Captain Bligh, sir, charged in that for a period o' bloody months 'e did mistreat the 'ands to the point of mutiny – '

'Put a sock in it, Able Seaman Fossett.'

Fossett stopped with his mouth open. He became aware of MAA Horner looming over him. In a harsh voice Horner said, 'Talk of mutiny, that's punishable by bloody death. Right?'

'Captain Bligh's mutiny, Master, not – '

'We all know who you meant, Able Seaman Fossett. And we all know you fancy yourself as a sea-lawyer. So watch it, all right?'

Fossett waited until the master-at-arms had moved on, taking it like a crab along the listed deck – big feet crushing hypothetical cockroaches as it was said of masters-at-arms and regulating POs by the lower deck – then he said, sotto voce, 'Daft bastard. We're all going to bloody snuff it before long.'

86

8

By NEXT morning the carrier seemed to be riding easier. She was still heavily listed but some of the nerve-racking lurching motion had gone.

Cameron went up to the for'ard end of the starboard walkway. Neil Grey was taking the watch: when Mason-Goodson had come to again during the night he had forgotten his order to Grey to remain by his side, had in fact seemed annoyed by his presence. There had been nothing further about 'Mr Christian'.

Grey reported, 'Wind's dropped a fraction, sir.'

'Yes.' The waves appeared to Cameron to be a shade less violent, though spume was still blowing from the crests and there was still the appearance of a white carpet laid across the sea's anger. But hope returned: any lessening of the gale was a very welcome sign and if the improvement continued they might yet come through.

But if they did, there was still a long way to go to the Virginia Capes and the sanctuary of Norfolk Navy Yard. And another point, one that would be on all their minds: when the weather moderated, the U-boat packs would be in a position to mount their attacks.

Cameron spoke of this to Grey.

'We'll be a sitting duck,' Grey said. 'No guns except the forty millimetres. Fat lot of good they'll be. And half of them won't be able to bear unless we can correct the angle of list.'

87

'We have the escort, Number One. In any case, there won't be any choice.'

'No.' Neil Grey gave a sigh and rubbed at tired, salt-rimmed eyes. 'It's a bugger. A real bugger. D'you think she can stay afloat at all?'

Cameron looked at Grey's drawn face. Grey was RNR, with a whole lot more experience of the sea, and ships, and ship construction, than he had himself. Cameron's father had himself been RNR: Cameron knew the breed. He said, 'I'll throw that question back at you, Number One. What do you think?'

Grey paused before answering. Then he said slowly, 'I don't like the feel of her. As though she's died already . . . waiting for burial. I can't see her lasting right through to Norfolk.'

'But surely . . . having lasted this far, when the gale's blown itself out . . . she'd have gone already if she was going to, wouldn't she?'

'It doesn't follow. We've not overcome the flooding of the compartments yet. What's the word from the tiller flat? Anyone been down?'

'Malling has. Not too good.'

Cameron believed that matters should improve, when at last the real weight went out of the gale, if they could at least get the shattered remains of the aircraft up from the hangar and over the side. That would take a lot of the list off her, relieving the port side of its deadweight of useless aircraft engines and wheels and body framework. That, however, couldn't be done yet. And what Grey had said was far from reassuring. Cameron had a hope that the *Queen Mary* would be making a report when she reached the Clyde – there was still the chance that her Officer of the Watch or lookouts had seen the wallowing carrier as the great liner had raced past. If that report was made, it was a fair hope that ocean-going rescue tugs would be sent out. But by the time those tugs could reach the position as reported by the *Queen Mary*, they would have been pushed and heaved by the force of the waves many miles away and a search could well prove abortive. The carrier's transmitting and receiving aerials had gone with the bridge superstructure and they were out of communication with the world beyond. Not that the breaking of wireless silence could be allowed . . . and Cameron knew that the senior officer of the destroyer escort wouldn't take the risk of homing enemy submarines onto the ships. So no assistance would be given to the searching tugs in their efforts to find them.

There was, of course, one other hope: a tow from the escort. But that was as yet one of the imponderables: the carrier, even though not one of the big ones, would be a heavy tow for small destroyers and an unmanoeuvrable one to say the least in hands not accustomed to ocean rescue.

In the tiller flat, now unmanned, the water level was closing in slowly on the steering engine, overcoming the pumps. Cameron had ordered periodic checks and these had been carried out by Chief PO Malting and Lieutenant(E) Tapp, together with an engine-room artificer from the ship's own complement. They'd had nothing happy to report; but, apart from the actual weight of water that could affect stability, the matter was not crucial. Not currently, since the ship was in any case unable to steer her way out of the trough. It would be a different story when the gale had blown itself out. Cameron asked how long it would take for the steering engine to be overhauled and put back into action.

'Depends,' Tapp said.

'On what?'

'A lot of things.'

'Can you spell them out?'

'No, I can't. I can't spell out hypothetical damage.'

'But surely – '

'There's no surely about it, sonny.' Tapp was a man in his middle forties, an engineer from the Merchant Service who had no love for the RN and disliked being under RN command.

And here was a Saturday afternoon sailor, still wet around the ears, quizzing him on his own professional ground. 'You'll just have to be bloody well patient till I've been able to strip the engine down and examine it.'

With that, Cameron had to be content. But he marvelled at the sheer obstinacy of an obviously bolshie man who was prepared even in current life-or-death circumstances to assert his bloodyminded independence.

The muttering about the Captain continued. It continued with a total lack of point. They were stuck with the results of Mason-Goodson's action in following a hunch successfully and there was nothing they could do about it.

A report of the murmurs of discontent reached Cameron via Master-at-Arms Horner. 'It's being stamped on, sir, never fear.'

'By you, Master?'

'Me and my RPOS, sir, will be watching out. For a start, I'm leaving it to the older 'ands, sir. The three-badge men very largely.'

'You're saying the trouble's with the younger men?'

Horner nodded. 'That is so, sir, yes. The hotheads. You know what they are, sir.'

Cameron did. He recalled his time at HMS *Royal Arthur*, the training establishment at Skegness, that had in peacetime been a Butlin's holiday camp, where he had done his time as an ordinary seaman before being recommended for his RNVR commission. After six weeks training, the newly joined ratings were allowed their first weekend leave, Friday to Sunday. On the Thursday, that leave had been cancelled. They didn't know it at the time, but the British Army was being withdrawn, heroically, from the Dunkirk beaches, and the whole nation was standing to. Cameron's messmates had held protest meetings in the manner of shoreside trade unionists, urging a deputation to the Captain, some of them even going so far in their ignorance as to suggest they went on strike until the grievance had been met. They hadn't known the Navy. They were put wise by their instructor, a seasoned petty officer with three good-conduct badges and a wealth of experience of young ratings behind him.

'Daft bunch o' bleedin' little twerps,' he'd said scathingly. 'Don't know you're born yet, you lot don't. You're talking mutiny, that's what you are. Take my word for it. If it reaches the Captain, he'll be entitled to shoot the bleedin' lot o' you. And another thing: to put in a complaint or request on behalf of anyone apart from just the one man named on the request form – round robin if you like – that's an act of mutiny in itself, see? Just piss off and forget it. Won't get you nowhere anyway, other than Detention Quarters – that's if the skipper lets you live.'

It had been largely bullshit, but it had worked.

No doubt something similar would work again, Cameron thought. As the MAA had said, the old stripeys would put the younger element wise.

They did; and amongst those who helped was one Stripey Haslam, able seaman by substantive rate, seaman gunner in his non-substantive, or specialist, rate. Haslam was a reliable old sea-daddy, old being a relative term at sea; at forty-eight aboard a ship where the average age was no more than around twenty-three, Stripey Haslam was indeed very old. He was a ponderous man, heavy but not tall; he ran to a good deal of fat around the stomach. He was slow-moving and had a slow way of speaking. What he said made sense and he was listened to as a seadog of much experience of the Navy, which he had joined as a seaman boy second class in the training establishment HMS *Ganges* at Shotley in Suffolk. One of his horrors in those early days had been the obligatory climbing of the immense mast that rose to the heavens from the concrete of the parade ground. That mast had been rigged as the mainmast of one of the old sailing men-o'-war, complete with yards and footropes, ratlines, and a fighting-top which could be reached either by way of the futtock shrouds or via what was known as the lubber's hole. The proper way, the only way for a man who aspired to be a seaman, was up the futtock

shrouds, which meant a climb leaning backwards and out-
wards from the ropes, suspended by fingers and bare toes
above the parade ground, until the victim could pull himself
over onto the boards of the maintop. The lubber's hole was
just that: a hole in the maintop through which you could climb
straight and upright from the ratlines. It was a narrow hole
and had Haslam been as fat then as he was now he would
probably have jammed. As it was, he used it on his first
attempt at the mast.

He was bawled out by the PO instructor. 'You there –
Haslam. Down you come, lad.'

He'd climbed down, shaking. He'd disobeyed an order:
they had been told to use the futtock shrouds. He was sent
up again and once more his nerve failed him. After that, it
was a case of Commander's Report as a defaulter. The
Commander was a fair man and instead of sending him
before the Captain for punishment he had given him a
second chance, spelling out what would happen if he failed
again: a caning followed by stoppage of leave until he went
up the futtock shrouds.

He was telling this story aboard the *Charger* as the bolshie
element moaned about Mason-Goodson. One of them asked,
'What did you do, Stripey?'

'What did I do? What I 'ad to do, that's what I did, climbed
them perishin' futtock shrouds, not wanting me arse cut to
ribbons and me leave stopped. Screwed up me courage, see.
And the next time it wasn't as bad, and then it come easy.
Anyway, what I bin trying to say is, you can't beat the Navy,
can't beat the system. It's built to beat you, see? You never
get away with nothing, not in the Andrew you never. So you
just takes it as it comes and you come up the other side. All
right? So don't go and do anything daft. And don't listen to
that Fossett and his daft ideas. He'll just get you into trouble
and take care to skate out from under 'isself, you mark my
words. Anyway – we're all in this together. All dependent on
each other, see?'

It might have helped; but the feeling throughout the ship

was unhappy. The skipper was three parts round the bend and that Cameron was an unknown quantity.

Later that day there was a marked improvement in the weather. The wind had dropped with surprising suddenness and with it the spume had vanished from the wave crests, although the waves themselves were still high and the carrier still lurched and sagged and rose again sluggishly as the sea passed beneath and lifted her only to drop again. But now there was hope in the air. When the sea flattened they could do something about the trim.

Cameron conferred with Chatterton, Grey and the two chief petty officers, Malting and Stoner.

'First thing is, clear away the debris, sir,' Malting said.

Cameron agreed. 'And get the water out, Cox'n. Then we can try to turn her into what's left of the wind. That depends on the steering engine, of course – we may still have to steer by pulley-hauley.'

'A tow, sir?' Stoner suggested. 'The escort – '

'I'll contact the senior officer just as soon as we can re-establish vs communication.' The escort was out of sight at the moment. That was not surprising in the circumstances; the gale had done its work of scattering the ships very effectively. In the meantime Cameron was faced with other difficulties. As reported now by the PMO, who had joined the deck party, a number of the hands were suffering from the effects of long exposure to cold and wet without adequate food. There were, MacAllister said, a number of injuries as well: cuts going septic, bad bruising, a number of fractures to limbs. The sick bay staff were coping, but only under great difficulty; and the seaman complement was going to be depleted, likewise the engine-room.

'Then it'll be a case of all fit hands,' Cameron said, steadying himself against the lurch of the steel deck. He turned to Stoner. 'Pass the word, please, chief. As soon as we're riding easier I'll want a muster of all daymen – cooks,

stewards, writers, supply assistants – the lot. They'll all work as seamen for as long as they're needed.'

And God help us all, Stoner thought to himself. The men known collectively as miscellaneous ratings were a cack-handed lot in his view, didn't know a fairlead from a fried egg, but they'd have to cope somehow. And since they had to, they would. He'd see to that personally.

'The Commander,' Mason-Goodson said in a pettish tone, 'has not reported to me as ordered. Have him found at once.'

'I'm sorry, sir. The Commander was lost overboard, along with – '

'Who're you?'

'Cameron, sir. Taking passage . . . I've assumed command for the time being, in the absence of – '

'What rubbish. I do not believe the Commander has been lost, I believe he is skulking. D'you hear me – *skulking*. I shall have him Court-Martialled. A report will go the Admiralty. . . .' Mason-Goodson's voice seemed to drift away, and his eyes closed. A few moments later they opened again. 'What has happened to my ship? Will somebody tell me that?'

Cameron took a deep breath. He didn't believe that much, if anything, would penetrate, but he did his best. After just a few words it became obvious that Mason-Goodson was not listening. Saliva began drooling from a corner of his mouth as he interrupted. 'It is all part of the plan against me. The plot . . . to discredit me. The Commander is a jealous man, Cameron . . . is that your name?'

'Yes, sir.'

'God will have His revenge. The Commander will be destroyed by His wrath, Cameron, do you understand?'

'Yes, sir.'

'I am the Captain of this ship. I have decided to alter course . . . to return to British waters and lay my complaints . . . to the proper authorities. Wear ship, Cameron. That is an order.'

94

'Aye, aye, sir.'

Cameron turned away, feeling immensely sorry that any captain should come to this in front of his ship's company. It was impossible to get through to him, the attempt was simply a waste of time. Behind him as he moved away Mason-Goodson began singing. It was a hymn: the naval hymn, for those in peril on the sea. It could hardly be more appropriate. The Captain's voice came out clear and strong, and after a pause of something like embarrassment the unexpected happened. The hymn was taken up by every man in the hangar.

> 'O hear us when we cry to Thee
> For those in peril on the sea . . .
> When Thy voice the waters heard
> And ceased their raging at Thy word. . . .'

Cameron found it very moving.

As he sang himself, there was a shout from the officer on watch at the fore end of the starboard walkway.

'Vessel in sight, bearing red two-oh, distant about two miles!'

The singing had stopped as the excited voice had cut into it. Cameron went fast for the ladder.

The distant ship was not easy to identify; she dipped constantly into the troughs of the waves, became totally obscured. Cameron watched closely through his binoculars as she rose briefly and he believed he caught a sight of the White Ensign. And a moment later a lamp began flashing from her bridge until once again she vanished behind the crests.

9

'SALVATION,' MR Fielder, Gunner RN, said. He was speaking to Mr Trimby. From the walkway Cameron had shouted down for a signalman and when the other vessel once again became visible the signalman was able to read off the brief series of flashes from an Aldis lamp.

'Making her letters, sir. It's *Invergarry*, sir.'

The word had spread fast. There had been a cheer from the hangar. Spirits rose: they were going to come through; *Invergarry* would stand by them. Even if they had to abandon, rescue would be at hand with scrambling nets and boats – provided they didn't have to go over into the drink just yet. The weather was still the predominant, deciding factor. In the sea that was still running they wouldn't have a hope.

Mr Trimby voiced these thoughts to the gunner. 'Depends how long we can last, eh?'

'We've made it this far,' Mr Fielder said with assurance, 'and we're going to come through, all right. Feel it in me bones,' he added. 'Felt it at Jutland.'

Mr Trimby raised an eyebrow. 'You in that lot, then?'

'Battle-cruiser squadron o' the Grand Fleet. Under Beatty. In the old *Lion*.'

Trimby had mostly missed the last war himself, joined in 1917 and spent what was left of the war as an apprentice artificer under training in a shore establishment, hadn't gone to sea till after the armistice. He'd been somewhat chagrined

96

about that, but was happy enough to have missed Jutland. So many ships sunk, so many men dead or badly wounded and badly burned when the shells of the German High Seas Fleet had taken out the gun turrets of the British battleships and battle-cruisers, or penetrated the armour plating over the magazines and shell-handling rooms, so many men drowned aboard their own ships as the orders had come from the bridges to flood the great steel tunnels that led down from the main deck to the handling rooms . . . tunnels over which the hatch covers were always clamped down hard during action, tunnels from which there was no escape.

By all accounts, Jutland had been hell.

Mr Trimby was suffering a degree of hell now and never mind the salvation that the gunner had spoken of. There would be things almost worse than death to face when he got back eventually to UK. The recent past might even catch him up in the States, probably would. There would be letters from solicitors and there would be the problems of alimony and the division of what had been their joint possessions in the home and he would no doubt be homeless. Mr Trimby didn't really know about these things, but he reckoned Maud would get the sympathy of the judge when it came to the divorce. You couldn't very well explain in open court, with all the lawyers in their wigs and whatnot, all the spectators and coppers and court attendants, that it had really all been Maud's fault because she didn't like doing it except for once a year on their wedding anniversary – if he happened to be at home and not in bloody Hong Kong or somewhere – when under protest she used to oblige. Oblige! Once a bloody year. Probably the judge wouldn't believe it in any case, so it would be a waste of time apart from being very embarrassing.

Invergarry had moved in closer, but not much closer: the sea was running too high for any close approach to be safe. But communication was established manually: all the carrier's signalling equipment had gone with the bridge superstructure. As the messages of enquiry came from the destroyer,

Cameron's yeoman of signals made the answers by hand semaphore from the walkway.

Cameron passed a report, as briefly as possible, of the conditions aboard. Currently the ship was stable and matters should improve when the weather moderated further. At the moment he was not in need of assistance. That could change if anything should happen suddenly. The destroyer reported herself shipshape though there had been a number of injuries to her company in the heavy seas. Cameron signalled an enquiry as to whether *Invergarry's* wireless had picked up any transmission indicating the sending of ocean-going rescue tugs from home.

The answer came back: No.

'*Queen Mary* couldn't have seen us,' Cameron said.

Grey shrugged. 'Either that, or they've had too many calls. The tugs, I mean. An escort carrier on a non-operational assignment, no squadron embarked . . . we wouldn't rate all that high, perhaps. They could be leaving us to the escort.'

Grey could be right. The overall view of the war at sea from the Admiralty would obviously be very different from that aboard a ship wallowing in the North Atlantic. In short, they could be expendable, which was an unhappy thought. Further signalling indicated that the other two destroyers of the escort had not reappeared after the scattering effect of the storm, had in fact been out of contact for the last thirty-six hours.

They were still very much alone, still lay helpless and naked to any attack by Hitler's forces.

Cameron went down the ladder to tell the ship's company what was going on. First he went across to where Mason-Goodson was still lying in the Neil Robertson stretcher, which was covered by a tarpaulin. An SBA was by his side. Cameron asked how the Captain was making out: he was currently sleeping, he saw.

'Rambling when he wakes, sir.'

'About anything in particular?'

'No, sir. Mumbles, mostly. Can't make any sense, not really. And he's getting weaker. Not taking nourishment. I reckon there's something on his mind, sir.'

'Yes,' Cameron said. That was all. He would get a detailed report from the PMO, who, he saw, was currently busy with splints and dressings, doing what could be done for the men with broken limbs. He was working with very inadequate resources, the contents of his surgery having been largely smashed during the violent rolling of the ship earlier, or rendered useless by the seawater that had poured down from the flight deck to penetrate the alleyways and compartments below the hangar.

Cameron saw that everyone was looking at him, waiting for some word of comfort.

'We'll come through,' he said, lifting his voice. 'As soon as the sea decreases I'll make the attempt to turn the ship north. After that, we'll ride easier and we can start to clear up the mess. If it becomes necessary, I'll take a tow from *Invergarry*. If she can't move us through the water at any speed, at least she'll keep our head to wind and sea. And that,' he added, 'is all I can tell you for now.'

He went below to the tiller flat, deserted since his order to bring the men up to the hangar. He took Chief PO Stoner with him. On the way down they collected Chatterton and Tapp.

Stoner was still worrying about his old parents. Stoner didn't entirely share Cameron's certainty that they were going to come through, though he'd put a good face on things so as not to spread alarm. If the carrier went, she'd be likely to go suddenly and a number of men were going to be trapped in her death throes. Those who survived wouldn't find rescue by the destroyer all that easy. There was still a big sea running and even when the gale had blown itself right out, that sea would remain for a while as a hangover and there would be a nasty swell in addition. Boatwork wouldn't be anyone's idea of a picnic and there would be hazards in the business of swimmers attempting to grab hold of the destroyer's scrambling nets. Stoner had been aboard a cruiser that had been sunk earlier in the war, in the Med which was by no means always a nice, flat, blue millpond. When Stoner's cruiser had gone down, having struck two mines not far off Pantellaria, which was in enemy occupation, there had been a gale blowing and the Med was as bleak as anywhere else could be under gale conditions. Not nice at all, and dead cold when Stoner had been projected into the sea along with many others. A destroyer had stood by just as *Invergarry* was doing now, and she had lowered her scrambling nets for the survivors to climb like flies up her shallow sides to the safety of the upper deck. It was all right in theory; in practice that destroyer had been rolling her guts out and several of the men had been flung forcefully against her steel plates by the waves. Stoner had seen a good mate of his, the chief yeoman of signals, get his head split open like a coconut against a projection in the ship's side, and then sink like a brick.

Out here in mid-Atlantic, the conditions were a lot worse, a lot worse even now, with the weather having moderated.

His parents – if he should go, what then? There might be some sort of pension payable to the parents of a son who'd been their sole support; again there might not. Stoner wasn't too sure though he'd made enquiries soon after the war had started. He'd asked the chief writer of the ship he'd been in, and the chief writer hadn't been sure and had made enquiries of the paymaster commander who hadn't known either. Back in RNB Stoner had enquired from the families' welfare people, and they'd been vague. It was possible legislation would be enacted . . . but even if there was to be a pension, it would be pretty niggardly, Stoner thought.

It was a worry, but it had to be put behind him.

With Cameron and the two engineer officers, Stoner went below to the tiller flat, right down low in the ship, right down aft. The jaws of hell, Stoner thought fancifully, the final trap.

The depth of water had increased despite the continuous use of the pumps and it was encroaching on the steering engine. Cameron asked, 'What d'you think, chief?'

'A long job,' Chatterton answered. 'And no good even starting till the compartment's dried out.'

'Which it won't, by the look of it.'

'No. Not till the stability's restored at any rate. That should help.'

Cameron, with Stoner, left the tiller flat and climbed back to the hangar deck. 'Bit of a stench down there, sir,' Stoner said warningly. 'All that dirty water . . . some of it bilge water, I reckon.'

'We'll get a report from the shipwright,' Cameron said. The shipwright's party had been sounding round almost continuously. The reports had been of water still entering the ship but not to dangerous proportions. So far. But Cameron hadn't liked the depth of water in the tiller flat. Neither, though he hadn't specifically stressed it, had the lieutenant-commander(E).

Cameron buttonholed Neil Grey and Chief PO Malting. He said, 'It's time to try to make the turn and restore stability, Number One.'

'Turn her by pulley-hauley?'

'Not that alone. I'm going to ask *Invergarry* to drop down on us, and try to pass a tow. Just to pull us round and out of the troughs. That's the first thing.'

'Tricky,' Grey said.

'Very tricky – I know, Number One. But I'm going to try it.' Cameron turned to Stoner. 'I'll want your most experienced hands in the fo'c'sle. What's your cable party like?'

'Some green, some not, sir. I can back up with some of the three-badge men from the quarterdeck division.'

Cameron nodded. 'Do that, buffer. And pass the word for all hands to stand by, prepare to tow for'ard. And a message to the engineer officer in the tiller flat: stand by main engines. We're going to move out.'

Grey had asked, what about Father? Cameron's answer had been that at last sight Mason-Goodson had seemed incapable of understanding anything that was going on around him.

'His ship still, you know.'

'In a – '

'If anything happens . . . if you lose the ship, will you have Admiralty backing?'

Cameron gave a short laugh. 'I don't know, Number One. Who can predict the Admiralty at the best of times? But Mason-Goodson is out for the count and it's up to us – up to me as it turns out. What I'm suggesting is all I can see to do, and I'm going to do it, Mason-Goodson or no Mason-Goodson.'

Grey said, 'Well, I'm right behind you. Just thought I ought to mention it, that's all, sir.'

Cameron clapped him on the shoulder. 'Quite right, Number One. And – thanks for your support. I'm going to need all the moral support I can get.'

The task was in fact a daunting one. To haul fifteen thousand tons of aircraft-carrier round into the still high waves, with her main steering gone and her innards soggy with seawater, and a dangerous list that couldn't be corrected until she had turned, was no small matter. If anything should go wrong, Mason-Goodson, whatever his physical and mental condition, might very well make hay of an RNVR officer when the matter came before the Board of Admiralty and the Chief of the Naval Staff. The staff, composed for the most part of elderly men, crusted admirals not, in Whitehall, wet with salt water, men who had all the time in the world to ponder and make decisions that had often to be made in minutes, if not seconds, by those out at sea . . . those shorebound old men could bring anyone's career to an abrupt and inglorious end. And the straight-striped RN stuck together. Mason-Goodson, if his mental state improved, and there was nothing to say it wouldn't, would be backed to the hilt. To lose an aircraft-carrier at a critical stage of the war in the North Atlantic – Britain's life-line for the supply of American troops, munitions and other war equipment – would not be popular.

That was something that had to be accepted now.

*

The signals had been made to *Invergarry*. The destroyer would co-operate but her commanding officer's reply contained a note of caution. The manoeuvre held great risk; and if his own ship became endangered he would slip the tow and perhaps make another attempt when the height of the waves had decreased further. In fact, in the exchange of signals, he had queried Cameron's decision not to delay a while; but appeared to have been convinced by Cameron's insistence that the carrier was unable to make good her steering engine until the ship had been turned and her list corrected.

Invergarry's final signal had been to wish Cameron good luck and a safe turn. Immediately upon receipt of this Cameron had ordered the cable and side parties to muster on the fo'c'sle and had sent word, by means of a chain of men passing the orders along to the sound-powered telephone in the hangar, to the engine-room that he would be in need of the main engine at short notice. Chatterton received this message on the starting platform and passed the word via Lieutenant(E) Tapp to the boiler-room, where the boilers, which had been allowed to die down earlier, had now been flashed up again. Chatterton knew that there was likely to be a good deal of manoeuvring of the engines as Cameron tried to force the ship round to a safe, or anyway a safer, heading. Instant response was going to be needed from the starting platform. It was all going to be made the more difficult by the fact that there was no instant communication between Cameron and the engine-room: chains of men were not exactly the fastest means of transmitting orders.

Tapp came back to report the boilers ready, all of them connected up to the system to produce the maximum steam pressure when required. Tapp's progress across the engine-room deck had been a sort of sideways lurch, like a pregnant duck, Chatterton thought. He was having difficulty himself in remaining upright on the starting platform, holding fast to the guardrail and hoping for the best: the best being that their single screw would bite the water and not race as the ship began to come round. The heavy list that the carrier was experiencing meant that the screw had lifted and was only just beneath the surface.

Chatterton was aware of the thump of his heart as they all awaited the first movement order from the walkway far above.

The destroyer had started her closing manoeuvre, moving dead slow astern to bring her counter inching towards the canted fo'c'sle of the carrier, two men ready with heaving lines to cast across the gap of water.

On *Charger*'s fo'c'sle deck, below the overhang of the flight deck above, the cable party waited in varying degrees of anxiety. Stoner was on edge, knowing very well what the risks were. With him, and in overall charge, was Neil Grey. Neither of them had done a similar job before, though both had some experience of being in a ship where a tow had had to be passed. Both knew the technics of the job, knew how it should be done properly – the hanging off of a bower anchor aboard the ship to be towed, the connecting of the towing vessel's steel-wire hawser to the cable, and then the veering of the cable as the towing ship took up the slack, after which the strain, and the tow, would be taken by the Blake slips and the bottle-screw slips as well as the brake of the capstan, or windlass in the case of *Charger*. All very straightforward, at least in theory.

This, however, was no ordinary tow. Neither Grey nor Stoner had handled, or even seen, a tow that was supposed to turn a heavy, virtually helpless ship from an Atlantic wave-trough, back into the teeth of wind and sea. And the circumstances were such that it was not possible to hang off an anchor. The towing pendant, once aboard, would have to be taken to the bitts on the port and starboard sides of the fo'c'sle and made fast. The hope had to be that the bitts would take the weight.

One of the three-badgemen brought in from the quarter-deck was Stripey Haslam. Haslam had once been in the cable party aboard a cruiser that had been dry-docked in Gibraltar, when the Commander had taken advantage of the dry-docking to order the ranging of the cable for inspection on the dock bottom. A rope known as a messenger had been made fast to the cable as it was lowered from the drum of the capstan. There had been a nasty accident when the cable had taken charge because of the actions of a cack-handed twit at the capstan. A young ordinary seaman, also cack-handed or in his case cack-footed, had managed to do what no good seaman ever did, and that was to place his foot in the bight of the messenger just before it ran away behind the tremendous weight of the cable. The youngster had been dragged with the speed of light along the deck and down the hawse pipe. He had jammed in the pipe itself and the leg that had caught the messenger had been pulled from its socket to land bloodily in the dock bottom. The other had caught the lip of the hawse pipe and had been forced up and down the man's body, broken off at the hip. It had, in fact, been this leg that had caused the jamming.

Stripey Haslam knew just what damage could be done on ships' fo'c'sles. . . .

Now, awaiting events, huddled into his oilskin and duffel-coat, he watched the green hands, so many of them hostilities-only men. If anything went wrong . . . it didn't bear thinking about. Lieutenant Grey and the buffer would have their work cut out, just a leading seaman and maybe half a dozen ABS who wouldn't get in a flap, or shouldn't. Stripey Haslam turned his mind to other things: a week or two in the States if they came through this lot, a bit of freedom until they were on draft for the UK and another ship. A week of booze and popsies – he wasn't too old for that, far from it.

His last bit of stuff, in fact, had been back in Greenock, a day or two before sailing, a matter of only a week or so ago, though now it seemed like bloody years. Morag, her name had been; he'd picked her up in a pub filled with cigarette smoke and seamen from the ships at the Tail o' the Bank. Very Scottish she was, and a shade tiddly, as was Haslam himself after a few whiskies and chasers.

He'd caught her eye and bought her another drink. They'd squeezed together at the bar, in a corner at one end. There had been very close physical contact and Stripey Haslam had reacted.

'Something you want,' she said, giggling.

'That's right enough. You?'

'Same as you,' she said, and eyed him closely. 'Older men,' she said, hiccupping. 'Pardon.'

' 'S all right,' Stripey said gallantly.

'Know what it's all about. No cock-eyed fumbling. Get straight there.' She eyed him again, though muzzily, and took a sip at her glass. 'You look a sexy enough beast.'

Stripey Haslam had never been called a sexy beast before. It wasn't the sort of phrase his old woman down in Fareham had ever used, for one thing. For another, most of his expeditions ashore had been in foreign, or anyway Empire, ports and the preliminary conversations had been much briefer and of a very different nature. Mostly they'd been 'You want jiggy-jig' or 'My sister very good, very cheap, big bum' or once, in Londonderry – not quite foreign – 'It's gone up since the war, Jack, it's sixpence now.'

He'd been very flattered; sexy beast, that was really nice. Going on past form, he'd made a big mistake. 'How much?' he'd asked.

What he got was a slap across the face and Morag's swift departure. Well, he wouldn't be making that sort of mistake in Norfolk, Virginia. You live and learn . . . but it was nice to think back on it now and realize that she'd wanted him for his own sake and not for profit. Very nice, good for the ego. At his age, too.

His reverie was broken into. Chief PO Stoner's voice came. 'You there, Stripey. Look alive, stand by to take *Invergarry*'s heaving line. Move up to the bitts, pronto!'

'Coming, buff.' Stripey Haslam lumbered towards the bitts. The destroyer's stern was now within a cable's-length or so. A man stood ready with a heaving line coiled over his wrist. A moment later the monkey's fist at the end of the heaving line streaked across, giving weight to the thin rope, expertly aimed. Just as expertly, Stripey caught the line, went with it to the eyes of the ship and fed it through the bullring, then hauled in. Behind the heaving line came a heavier rope, a grass line. As the weight came on, the hands of the cable party tailed onto the line, backing Stripey up. The towing pendant came to the bullring and was pulled through, carried to the bitts and made fast. Casting a look around the fo'c'sle, Grey raised his voice to a shout towards the walkway where Cameron was waiting.

'*Tow passed!*'

There was a wave. 'Thank you, Number One.' Cameron turned to the signalman alongside him. 'Make by semaphone to *Invergarry*: tow secured. Am ready to proceed.'

Two minutes later a brief signal came from the destroyer and the towing pendant began to lift as the towing ship moved ahead.

Cameron said, 'Engine slow ahead. And pass to the tiller flat, rudderhead to hard-a-port.'

Then he began praying.

10

In the tiller flat the steering party under Chief Petty Officer Malting strained away, pulling their guts out in an attempt to force the big rudderhead over to port so that the blade would move to starboard and, with luck, bring the ship round as the towing vessel went ahead. If the carrier had been under main steering the order from the bridge would have been for full starboard wheel, and the connections of the steering system would have put the rudder blade over to starboard; but under pulley-hauley direct onto the rudderhead, the order had had to be as Cameron had given it: to port.

Ben Malting sweated and heaved with the rest, tailing onto the tackle that would, or should, pull the big blade round against the tremendous pressure of the sea. As, inch by inch, the rudderhead moved, they felt the beat of the engines. Cameron was now moving slow ahead to ease the tow as the destroyer began to haul the bows round to starboard.

At home now, in the office of the Flag Officer in Charge at Greenock, in the headquarters of the Commander-in-Chief Western Approaches, and in the Admiralty's Operations Room deep down in the bomb-proof bunker beside Horse Guards Parade, there was a degree of consternation. The North Atlantic, according to the meteorologists, was experiencing the worst weather for some forty years. The troop transport *Queen Mary*, arriving in the Firth of Clyde, had reported waves more than sixty feet in height, and a gale gusting to some 120 mph. The *Queen Mary* had reported something else: a big vessel wallowing and apparently helpless in the trough between two gigantic waves. The sighting had been brief; the visibility had been very poor and the class of the vessel had not been established beyond doubt but it was believed to have been an aircraft-carrier.

In Greenock, FOIC said, '*Charger*. So far as I'm aware she's the only carrier currently crossing. What was the given position, Raikes?'

Captain Raikes, Chief of Staff, repeated the position: this was a little off the normal wartime track and not far south of the Denmark Strait.

'Confirm with Admiralty,' FOIC said.

Raikes used the security line to the Operations Room. The confirmation came that *Charger* was indeed the only carrier in the North Atlantic. FOIC got on the line himself and spoke of ocean-going rescue tugs, from either the Clyde or Plymouth.

He was speaking to the Duty Captain. The answer was the one that Cameron had foreseen: *Charger* was currently non-operational. Ocean-going rescue tugs didn't grow on trees and such as were available must be held in readiness for possible succour of victims more essential to the conduct of the war: cruisers that might be torpedoed or mined, troop transports crammed to the gunwales with soldiers and loaded down to their marks with war materials – ammunition, field guns, tanks and armour – or tankers filled with vital oil fuel.

'There are men involved, Captain. Four hundred and more.'

'I know, sir.' The Duty Captain sounded dead tired, weary of war in all its forms, all its cruelties. 'I'm sorry, but those men can't be allowed to weigh. In any case, the value of an ocean-going tug would be limited in the current conditions – '

'Weather's damn well moderating,' FOIC barked, 'according to the latest report.'

'Yes, sir. But the sea's still very high. I – '

'D'you mean to say you're going to do damn all about it?'

There was a sound like a sigh. 'My hands are tied, sir. I'll put it to the First Sea Lord – he's due here shortly, with the Prime Minister. That's all I can do. We mustn't forget one thing: *Charger* may not be in difficulties at all. Just one glimpse from the bridge of the *Queen Mary* – '

FOIC cut him off brusquely by banging down the handset. He disliked being spoken to as though he were half-witted and he was furiously angry at what he considered the total disregard of so many lives.

'Damned buggers,' he said to Raikes, and lit a cigarette with fingers that shook. 'The human factor. . . .' His voice tailed off; however real the human factor, it didn't count in war. He was well enough aware of that. The families wouldn't be very happy with that outlook, though. His mind switched to a sudden thought about *Charger*'s captain. 'Mason-Goodson,' he said reflectively.

'Yes, sir?'

FOIC sat back in his chair, rested his gold-ringed cuffs on the desk. 'Difficult feller. I don't know . . . I'm just wondering how he's making out.'

'In what way, sir?'

'Oh, never mind, it was just a thought. Ring for my secretary, will you, Raikes. I believe I've got some sort of social tittery on my plate this forenoon. Provost of Greenock . . . War Weapons Week.'

Weapons were more important than men. Some men, anyway. And some families.

The families, naturally, knew nothing of what was taking place out there in the storm-torn North Atlantic wastes. In Queen Street, Portsmouth, Bessie Malting carried on with the neverending chores of running a pub without a husband handy. The night before there had been one of Goering's air raids on Pompey, mostly it had been North End that had got it, but there was damage elsewhere as well. Fratton had been hit, the railway station was out of action, as were the engine sheds. Kings Road in Southsea had virtually vanished and the fires from the incendiaries were burning still. Some of the warehouses in the dockyard had been hit – not far from the old *Victory*, though by a stroke of luck she'd survived in her dry-dock, her Admiral's flag flying still.

Bessie's pub had had a fairly near miss and once again all the windows had been blown out. There was a tremendous mess to be cleared up but Bessie had opened on time. Her first customer was the off-watch gunner's mate of the Commodore's guard from the barracks. He lent a hand with sweeping up the last of the glass and general debris.

'It's an ill wind, Bess,' he said.

'Eh?'

'Ben missed this lot. We had incendiaries on the barracks, and the mess got it again.'

'I could do with Ben here right now,' Bessie said. She patted at her hair: last night's dust seemed to have got everywhere. 'There's times when I think a man's lucky to be off at sea rather than home.'

'Meaning the work, eh?'

'Not the work, though there's that too. Meaning that girl of ours. When Ben's away, she plays me up. Don't get away with much I can tell you, but it's a strain.' She paused again. 'Out till one a.m. night before last. I was that worried.'

The gunner's mate clicked his tongue. 'Too bad,' he said. 'If I was you I'd tan her bottom for her.'

Bessie didn't answer. She said in an unusually small voice, 'I'll be that glad when Ben gets home.'

Chief PO Stoner's parents, not far away as it happened in the Royal Portsmouth Hospital, would also be glad when their nearest and dearest got back safe to Pompey Town. Last night their home had been destroyed, burned to the ground by the incendiaries. They had only just about escaped death, taken from the very jaws of hell by an air raid warden and some seamen ashore on night leave from the barracks. They had both suffered burns, not too serious but enough to put them both in hospital, where now they lay separated, one in the men's ward, the other in the women's, each worrying about the other and both worrying, as they always did, about their son. There was always danger out at sea and the citizens of Pompey knew all about the naval casualties; there was always, but always, a family mourning a husband, a father, a brother, a son. Pompey had had its share of war all right, more than its share. Now the old people both felt they couldn't take any more. They would be glad enough to go. But before that happened they wanted to see their son, just once again. Each in their separate ward, when their burns had been dressed though the pain continued, prayed that God would grant them that.

The families didn't even know about the appalling weather out in the Atlantic: in wartime, the authorities didn't offer any help at all to the Nazi *Luftwaffe*, not even by way of weather reports. Never mind that Berlin could be presumed to have its own meteorologists, you didn't give them confirmation or otherwise. So weather was on the secret list, unless you happened to be right underneath it. As was Mr Trimby's sister-in-law in one part of Wolverhampton, and Mr Trimby's lawful wife in another part.

It was raining cats and dogs in Wolverhampton. Blowing, too. Very unpleasant; Mr Trimby's sister-in-law had difficulty in holding her skirt down as she walked along the road – a man coming along the other way was taking a good look and she glared at him as he went past, grinning and giving her a wink.

'Cheek,' she said witheringly.

'Might see that an' all,' the man said, and when, after going on further, she glanced back over her shoulder, the man had also turned and was staring at her bottom. She gave a flounce and looked around for a policeman, but of course, as usual, there wasn't one. They appeared only when they weren't wanted. Like the day she'd been caught with Alf Trimby and there'd been all that stupid fuss.

The little episode of the Peeping Tom made her think again about Alf. She couldn't make up her mind about him. It looked as thought her sister Maud was heading for the divorce court. Where did that leave her? Marrying Alf Trimby? Well, she wasn't sure about that and anyway he hadn't asked her. Might not be interested in actual marriage; what they'd done . . . well, that had just been sex and that was different. Wasn't it? Animal instincts, a natural thing to do. Being married to Alf wouldn't be the same thing at all. In himself he was rather dull really, and being a sailor he'd be away an awful lot, which would mean long periods of no nookey. Anyway, whatever else happened, one thing was certain: she was going to be quoted as the whatsit, co-respondent.

In another equally wet and windy part of Wolverhampton, Maud Trimby sat in her mother's front parlour and listened to the old woman going on and bloody on about Alf, who, she said for perhaps the hundredth time, was the lowest of the low, equalled only by her other daughter.

'I'll never speak to 'er again,' she stated, again for the hundredth time. 'Not never I won't. She won't darken my doors again, just you see.'

Maud said nothing. There was no point, not with mum, who never listened anyway. Old Mrs Prendergast, widow of a man who'd worked all his life in the zinc industry until something had happened to his balance and he'd fallen into a tub of something or other, zinc probably, when Maud had been six years old, was built in the same sort of mould as Queen Victoria, even down to the black dress, widow's cap and all, and the stoutness. And the autocracy and much else besides. She was a layer-down of the law. And she was dead against divorce and lately had said so many times.

She was at it again. 'You've made your bed, Maud, now you must lie on it. That's God's will. I'll not 'ave this 'ouse sullied by any divorce. Not never I won't.'

'But what am I to do, mum? I've already wrote to that solicitor. Alf – '

Mrs Prendergast lifted a stick that lay handy on the settee. 'And another thing. I won't 'ave that dreadful man's name spoken in this 'ouse. Not never again. What your dear father would have thought I do *not* know, a God-fearing man like 'im who never did nothing wrong in 'is 'ole life, and up there twice every Sunday at St Peter's, worshipping on 'is knees. . . .'

She rattled on and on, like a tramcar that never arrived at the terminus. Maud grew restive. She'd heard a lot about dad over the years since his death, and she knew perfectly well how God-fearing he'd been without it being stressed again now. Which it was, while the stick was thumped on the floor. Maud began shaking and then said something she shouldn't have said. She said, 'God didn't bloody save him from the zinc, did He?'

Old Mrs Prendergast heard that, all right. She gasped and laid a hand on her heart. Her face went white. Breathing hard she said, 'Ooh, you wicked, wicked girl! What a blasphemous thing to say! I never did 'ear the like, I didn't. Perhaps the Lord'll do what's only right and proper in 'Is eyes and take that man to 'is everlasting torment. If what should 'appen does 'appen, 'e'll never again come back from sea.'

Maud was shattered. Tears flowed. Alf was rotten, she knew that, mum had said so and of course there was truth in it. That awful scene . . . Alf standing there, sheepish with his lack of trousers, her sister's nudity, she would never forget it. But–yes, there was a but. She'd been married to Alf a long while and some fondness of feeling remained in spite of it all. He would never do it again, she was sure of that. He had always been a humble man, and he'd been terribly embarrassed. But it was probably too late now. She didn't know much about solicitors but it was possible that once they'd been started as it were they couldn't be stopped, rather like a runaway horse.

'What's this about an aircraft-carrier?'

The speaker was the First Sea Lord. The Duty Captain answered. 'Question raised by FOIC Greenock, sir.' He explained.

'What's the disposition of rescue tugs? The Clyde, the Mersey, Plymouth? Portsmouth, perhaps?'

114

'There's an availability on the Clyde, sir. One tug. Another two in the Western Approaches – I've been in touch with C-in-C in Liverpool.'

The First Sea Lord nodded, and glanced at the Prime Minister who was seated in a chair, looking across at the large wall map showing the dispositions of the British and Allied fleets, together with what was known of the movements of the German, Italian and Japanese sea forces. Cigar smoke wreathed over the Operations Room. The First Sea Lord noted that the Churchillian gaze appeared to be directed more at the trim uniformed figures of the Wrens on duty with their pointers than at the chart itself. There was something like a grin on the cherubic features: the Prime Minister was a very human man . . .

'Weather's moderating,' the First Sea Lord said. 'Isn't that so, Captain?'

'Yes, sir – '

'Well, then! And those tugs could be required elsewhere at a moment's notice – action damage. And the report of *Charger* is very vague and in fact totally uncorroborated.' The First Sea Lord hummed and ha'ed for a while, then said, 'Masterly inactivity . . . we'll wait and see. What with conditions improving. . . .' Then he asked a question. 'Who's commanding *Charger*, do we know?'

'Yes, sir. Captain Mason-Goodson.'

'I see. And her executive officer?'

The Duty Captain had already checked the Navy List: this was something he always did whenever a warship was reported in difficulties; one could have served past commissions with the officers aboard. He said, 'Commander Warren, sir.'

'Don't know him,' the First Sea Lord said, 'but I know Mason-Goodson. I was snotties' nurse when he was a wart in the old *Dreadnought*. I hope Warren's a good man.'

The Duty Captain gave him a quick look; but nothing further was said.

*

The towing pendant was lifting from the water, starting to come up bar-taut between the two vessels, not a happy sign. The mid point of the tow should be just beneath the water. Cameron, watching closely from the walkway and hearing the shout from Neil Grey on the fo'c'sle, passed orders down to the engine-room.

'Engine to half ahead.'

'Engine to half ahead, sir.' The message was relayed down the line to the sound-powered telephone at the after end of the hangar. Cameron waited anxiously for the extra thrust to take some of the strain off the tow. He assumed that a reverse action would be taking place aboard the destroyer, and a moment later an Aldis lamp, flashing from *Invergarry*'s bridge, gave the confirmation. *Invergarry* had eased her engines to slack off the pendant. The tow continued; the men in the tiller flat used their beef and muscle to hold the rudderhead over across the force of the sea. Ben Malting, watching the gyro repeater, gave the straining seamen some comfort.

'She's moving over, lads. Just a little. Keep it up and we'll get there, all right?'

Just a degree or two as yet, but it was in the right direction and every degree counted. Safety – up to a point – and a more comfortable motion would come once they were round; and the steering, which would continue by pulley-hauley until the steering engine had been dried out and overhauled, would be that much easier.

In the engine-room Chatterton moved about, watching dials and gauges, watched the ratings as they went round all the bearings with their long-necked oil cans. The cant of the deck was alarming, growing worse than ever as the carrier put her shoulder to the sea, butting into it under her own power as well as under *Invergarry*'s pull. Chatterton spared a thought for the men aboard the destroyer. They would be having one hell of a time, their little tin can flung all over the place as it thrust into the waves, cutting slap through them probably, to emerge from submersion like a dog coming out of a pond, until it met the next onslaught, the next in the succession of waves marching in solid lines across – or so it seemed – the whole of the North Atlantic.

There was a slop of water across the engine-room deck, mostly gathering along the port side but tending to run across when the ship gave an inert-feeling lurch over to starboard. That water was deepening. Lieutenant(E) Tapp remarked on it.

'Can't go on for ever like this, chief.'

'Maybe we'll not have to. When she's righted – '

'That's all we ever hear,' Tapp said in his sour tone. 'When she's righted. Me, I doubt if she ever will. The feel's all wrong. Like she's died in the night. You can feel that for yourself, surely to goodness?'

'I don't like it,' Chatterton admitted, 'but we'll do what we can.' He noticed that Tapp was looking constantly up the network of steel ladders that led to the platform outside the airlock leading into the engineers' cabin alleyway, the airlock that was the only escape route from the engine-room if things went wrong. Tapp had the aspect of a man who would dearly have liked to place himself as close as possible to the airlock. The engine-room could become a death-trap if insufficient warning was given to evacuate. Often enough in war there was no time at all. Shells, torpedoes, in other waters mines, could take the engine spaces direct, and then it was all over. Tapp's nervousness was understandable. And not all catastrophes were attributable to enemy action: Chatterton had had a cousin who'd been chief engineer aboard another escort carrier where a fault had developed in the fuel system, the aviation spirit system for re-fuelling the aircraft of the Fleet Air Arm squadron. There had been a leak, or so it was assumed afterwards, in the refuelling pipes carrying that high-octane aviation spirit, and there had been a spark. That had been the end: there were no survivors. No one to tell what kind of hell had broken over the engine-room, but Chatterton had experience enough and imagination enough to see it for himself very clearly.

The cold, up there in the fore end of the starboard walkway, was still intense and Cameron and his signalman were wet through from the water coming in huge dollops over the lifted starboard side to wash down across the flight deck or to cascade over the men standing by the tow on the fo'c'sle. But cold though it was, Cameron found himself sweating beneath his oilskin as he watched the desperate fight of the carrier to come round into what was still an appalling sea. He could almost feel the tremendous strain the ship was under, feel it in his own body.

Feel it in his mind, too.

He had undertaken a tremendous responsibility, taken it all on himself. Maybe he had acted hastily; maybe he should have paid more heed to the caution implicit in the signals from the *Invergarry*. Maybe it would have been wiser to wait for the weather to moderate further.

Maybe he should at least have had words with Mason-Goodson. But there had seemed little point and he had believed inside himself that there was no time to waste, had believed the ship simply wasn't going to go on standing up to the punishment she was getting. Metal, especially welded metal, had a limit to its endurance – there had already been that splitting of the welded seam down the side of the hangar, a bad sign to start with. That could worsen and in fact it had, affecting welding elsewhere, in more vital parts. Hence the water that had been coming in.

In any case, it was done now. He and all aboard were committed. So were the men aboard the destroyer. There would be no about-turn now. It was a case of grin and bear it.

He was aware that the ship was turning, turning so very slowly that it was almost imperceptible. But so far, so good. Now she'd started she ought to go on. There was no reason, perhaps, why she shouldn't. The tiller flat was doing its stuff, the rudder had been reported fully round; there had been no racing of the screw and all was well in the engine-room. The tow had lifted but action had been taken in time. The ship was shouldering into the sea – protestingly, but she was beginning to make it. The signs were not too bad.

Sweating, Cameron prayed. He prayed with sincerity . . . wondered if Mason-Goodson was doing the same, if he was fully aware of what was going on, which most likely he was not.

Prayer, it seemed, was not being listened to this time. Cameron heard the sudden shout from the signalman beside him and turned sharply. The daylight seemed, suddenly, to be blotted out. High above the struggling ship, the father and mother of all wave-crests loomed in gigantic, grotesque threat. It was going to drop on them and there was nothing to be done about it. Cameron yelled an unnecessary warning to the fo'c'sle as the great crest began to curl over. As the wave fell, the ship gave a lurch, her bows lifting high in response to the heavy surge of water in the trough; the enormous weight of ton after ton after ton of solid water hit below the starboard for'ard edge of the flight deck. With the heavy port list still on the ship, the water took the flight deck at an angle, lifting the whole for'ard section and forcing it up and back, stripping it almost as far as what had been the barrier, the wire preventer that in normal times caught and held an aircraft that had made a bad landing and had overshot the round-down aft and missed the trip-wires with its hook.

The broken flight deck effectively blocked the view from the makeshift conning position in the walkway. And, lifted into the air like a great foresail, it immediately affected the handling of the ship.

The carrier's bows began to pay off to port. The tow was still in place, the destroyer appeared unaffected except insofar as she was also paying off to port under the great weight of the tow. With the flight deck thus lifted, water was smashing down into the hangar with every wave that dropped on her. There was chaos on the fo'c'sle: even the Blake slips had been buckled, the stock of the starboard anchor twisted half over the lip of the hawse-pipe and the windlass below the break of the fo'c'sle almost wrenched from its moorings in the deck. The bulwarks had gone, smashed flat, and with them, sent hurtling from the fo'c'sle by the sheer weight of the falling water, had gone two men, a leading seaman and an AB. There was no sign of them in the sea's grim turbulence and no hope whatever of a rescue.

Cameron had struggled his way down from the walkway, through the ship to the shattered fo'c'sle. Neil Grey had been thrown violently against the after guardrail and his left arm hung as limp as a rag doll's. But he was on his feet, clutching with his right hand onto a stanchion that had survived the wave's onslaught.

He said, 'The tow's intact, sir. Something of a miracle . . . but God knows what we do now.'

'We try again,' Cameron said.

'Do we? I don't know . . . I believe we should have made the turn to port, not starboard. It's not too late.'

They had been into that, and Cameron reminded Grey of the fact. 'Too risky, Number One. We can't risk being pooped.' For smashing weights of water to drop straight down onto the after section, the open deck below the round-down aft, could prove murderous, taking the ship down with all hands. That risk was still there. Any turn would have to be made to starboard, into the sea rather than attempting to run before it. Cameron was about to have the destroyer informed by semaphore that he intended proceeding with the tow when the towing pendant fell slack, its inboard end sagging down from the bullring while the carrier once again fell off the sea, lurching heavily to port and lifting soggily to the wave that dropped and then passed beneath her.

The tow had parted.

Now more than ever, they were in the sea's grip, entirely at its mercy. Cameron felt completely at a loss: did they try to pass another tow, and then perhaps face a repeat of what had already happened, sustaining more damage in the process, likely enough more casualties as well? Or did they lie there until the sea smashed them to pieces and drowned them all?

Cameron gave his head a shake, clearing it. The biting cold, the wet, the din of the sea as it hit the carrier's side again and again, making the hangar give off a booming sound like gunfire, the distant shriek of the wind as it tore across the crests – it seemed to inhibit thought. But, of course, there was only the one action, the one answer: they had to pass another tow.

Meanwhile *Invergarry* was signalling by Aldis lamp. Cameron's signalman was preparing to semaphore an acknowledgment when like a ghost, a spectre from some past life, Captain Mason-Goodson, free of the Neil Robertson stretcher and carried by his steward and another man, his legs with the broken ankles dangling, appeared alongside the windlass.

He seemed to be calling up to the fo'c'sle: his voice was thin, lost in the tearing racket of wind and sea. Cameron moved aft, holding on where he could, and dropped down beside the dishevelled figure of the Captain.

'In the name of the Holy Son of God,' Mason-Goodson said savagely, '*what are you doing with my ship?*'

11

MASON-GOODSON WAS wet through and shivering violently. His big face was almost purple, the blood vessels distended, as it seemed, by sheer rage. But he appeared to be in control of his senses and his tone had been sharp and incisive. Behind him Cameron saw the PMO and his number two, the surgeon lieutenant. The PMO seemed to have lost some of his assurance.

Mason-Goodson said, 'Well? I have asked you a question, Cameron. Kindly answer it.'

Cameron swallowed. 'I'm trying to save her, sir. Attempting to turn into wind and sea, out of the trough.'

'Are you, indeed? And making a damn poor job of it! I see the tow has parted.'

'Yes, sir. I propose to take up the tow again – '

'Do you indeed? I happen to be in command of this ship, Cameron. You and everyone else will take their orders from me, is that clear enough for you? If you refuse to obey my order, you will be placed in close arrest.'

Cameron hesitated. The Captain was showing no overt signs of any mental incapacity now, though it was a moot point whether a totally sane captain would speak of close arrest of an officer in current conditions of extreme emergency. Over Mason-Goodson's shoulder, as water cascaded down from another curling crest, Cameron caught the eye of the PMO. MacAllister lifted his shoulders in a hopeless shrug that told its own tale clearly enough: what the Captain did about his ankles in defiance of medical advice was his own affair; and MacAllister was not going to take the enormous risk of advising Cameron that Mason-Goodson was mentally unfit to resume command. And Mason-Goodson's next words were sane and competent enough.

'Report the state of my ship, Cameron. Engines, steering, seaworthiness, stability. And a full summary of the actual damage. Then send for the shipwright and the engineer officer.'

There was nothing else to be done. Cameron was forced to accept the position. Mason-Goodson ordered himself to be roped securely to a stanchion on the starboard side of the deck below the break of the fo'c'sle and under what had been the overhang of the fore end of the flight deck, now lifted like a sail. An empty whisky case from the wardroom stores, cast out into the for'ard lift well, was placed beneath him. On this he sat, with his plaster-covered ankles sticking wetly out in front. When all the reports were in, he gave his orders and gave them forcefully enough, no hesitation.

'The situation has altered.' He gestured upwards. 'The tearing back of the flight deck. With that protuberance, the ship won't turn to starboard into the sea, and into the full force of the wind as she crests the waves – if ever she does. The one thing to do is to turn away, make the turn not to starboard but to port. I – '

'We'll risk being pooped, sir. I did – '

'Kindly don't argue with me, Cameron. I know what I'm doing. I have been advised. . . .' Mason-Goodson didn't pursue that, didn't divulge the source of the given advice, but Cameron was able to make a guess. It was possible to argue mental unbalance in anyone who derived advice from on high, and if Mason-Goodson exhibited any strange tendencies later, it could be a lever for the PMO to pull, but not now. Mason-Goodson went on, 'I intend making the turn to port, but not yet. I believe the ship is riding it out and will not sink. Therefore I intend waiting until there's further moderation in the weather. Have *Invergarry* informed accordingly.'

Cameron tried again. 'The ingress of water, sir – '

'In the hangar, yes. I'm well aware of that, Cameron, and of the shipwright's report on the matter. Use your head, Cameron. Much of the inflow will go straight overboard again from the opened seam in the port side. If too much collects, then I'll have the seam opened further.'

Cameron had to admit that Mason-Goodson could have a point: with so much damage already inflicted by the sea, a little extra man-made damage couldn't make matters any the worse.

Naturally enough the news had gone round the ship's company within a couple of minutes: Mason-Goodson had resumed command and had given Lieutenant-Commander Cameron a bollocking. Mason-Goodson had never been popular; but now the lower deck was tending to split in its reaction. Mason-Goodson might be a bastard and was, but he was a Captain RN, whilst Cameron was RNVR. Mason-Goodson was in his middle fifties and had spent his life at sea since leaving the Royal Naval College at Osborne. He had been at sea right through the last lot and had quite likely been with the Grand Fleet at Jutland. He had, so said Stripey Haslam authoritatively, a sight more sea experience than had Cameron, who looked as if he was no more than twenty-three or four. Which was not to denigrate Cameron who had done pretty well so far. Pretty well, but he could have made the wrong decision through sheer lack of experience . . . the skipper seemed to think so, anyway. So which was the more likely to be right?

'We don't know, do we?' a supply assistant asked. 'Skipper, he's been acting funny, hasn't he? Direct line to God an' all that, I reckon – '

Stripey Haslam cut in. 'Supply assistants, Jack Dusties, bloody miscellaneous ratings, bloody daymen . . . bloody idlers they were rated as in the old sailing days, they don't 'ave no opinions on seamanship – right?'

'It's our lives,' the SA said stubbornly. 'I reckon we got a right to – '

'You don't 'ave rights in the Andrew, son, you 'ave *privileges* when you've earned 'em. So just put a sock in it an' – '

'I reckon we have a right to vote.'

Stripey Haslam stared in disbelief. '*Vote?*'

'Yes, vote. Vote on who we want as skipper. Like I said – it's our lives.'

'You must be off your bleedin' rocker, you lousy perishin' bloody little bolshie! Vote my arse! What you're talking is bloody *mutiny*, an' if the jaunty 'ears you, you'll be in bloody cells.'

Ben Malting was aware of the undercurrent and it placed him in a dilemma. As he remarked to Mr Fielder, destined to be the gunner of the *Veracity*, he couldn't say anything about Mason-Goodson, it wasn't his ship, it wasn't his place, and he wouldn't encourage any such talk as was going on. But he knew from his past experience of Lieutenant-Commander Cameron that he was a first-rate seaman and a very dependable officer.

'I reckon we're safe in his hands, sir,' he said to the gunner. 'I'd like to get that across to those bleeding doubters. To hear some of 'em talk, you'd think they believed Mr Cameron was responsible for the mess we're in now.'

'Leave it, 'Swain,' the gunner advised. He was trying to light his pipe but without success. Even inside his oiled-silk pouch, the tobacco was damp. 'You can't make any difference to what blokes have made up their minds to believe. And as you said yourself, you can't criticize the skipper. Not even seem to.'

Malting nodded. Mr Fielder was right enough: best leave it. The skipper was in command now and that was that. Malting, a long service PO, by his very nature shied away from anything that might even remotely be construed as a mutinous thought, and if Mason-Goodson ever got wind of anything of that sort, there would be mighty trouble. He would be better employed, along with all other chiefs and POs, in giving full actual and verbal backing to the skipper.

The ship remained in the trough, broadside to the sea. She rolled and lurched heavily and water continued to drop down by way of the lifted flight deck. That sail-like protrusion, as the height of the waves continued slowly to grow less, caught the westerly wind and tended to slew the ship to port. It became obvious that to that extent Mason-Goodson had been right: in the new conditions it would very likely be impossible to turn her to starboard.

Life was now almost unbearably uncomfortable. The starter engine activating the pumps had packed up owing to the inflow of water below, and all hands had been organized by Chief PO Stoner into watches to operate the pumps manually; exhaustion soon set in to men who were constantly soaked and had not enough hot food to keep them fit for heavy work. But somehow they stuck at it, as did the hands on the tiller flat, also working in set watches. The grumbling was intense and bitter, the lower-deck feud continuing as between Mason-Goodson and Cameron. The factions were split fairly evenly. In the end the petty officers and leading hands, tired out themselves, left them to it. The feeling in the ship worsened. The master-at-arms reported to Cameron.

Cameron was inclined to leave it alone. There was no action he could take without exacerbating matters.

'A pep talk, sir,' the jaunty suggested. 'A warning about loose chat.'

'I don't think so, Master. The very fact of doing that . . . it would bring it straight to the Captain's attention.'

'Better that than let it go on, sir. Ought to be nipped in the bud if you ask me, sir.' The master-at-arms was one of those who believed in age and experience over youth: he was not that young himself, and tight discipline was his life. In the old days of the sailing navy, before his own time admittedly, someone would have been flogged by now, fifty or so lashes, tied down to the gratings.

But Cameron wouldn't budge. He said so, flatly, and the master-at-arms saluted and turned away. He remarked later to his subordinate, the regulating petty officer, that in his opinion Cameron was hoping to take over again from the Captain. 'Bit of an upstart,' he said. 'And playing with fire.'

'How's that, then, eh?'

The jaunty laid a finger alongside his nose. 'A wink's as good as a nod,' he said sotto voce. The penny dropped in the RPO's mind: Cameron, by his non-action, was encouraging the anti-Mason-Goodson faction, hoping to benefit. That, too, could be considered mutinous. Of course, officers didn't mutiny . . . or did they? The RPO had naturally been aware of the buzz that the skipper, lying in the hangar, had addressed one of the officers as Mr Christian. Mr Christian of the *Bounty* had most definitely mutinied, hadn't he? Funny, that. Maybe the skipper had had another of his premonitions. . . .

As dusk came down that day there was a signal from *Invergarry*: a vessel had been sighted, bearing south-westerly, as yet around four miles distant. *Invergarry*, as the so far unknown vessel had dipped between the rollers in fading light, had made the challenge of the day and still awaited the identification.

This was reported to Mason-Goodson in his position below the break of the fo'c'sle.

'Well?' he said shortly. 'What's *Invergarry* doing about that?'

'Don't know, sir,' the signalman said.

'You don't know? I'll damn well tell you what she *should* be doing, then. She should be opening fire. The Admiralty Fighting Instructions state that if the challenged vessel fails to respond *immediately* with the correct reply, then the challenging vessel's duty is to open fire. You understand?'

'Oh – yessir.'

'Good. Go away, then, and report further signals immediately on receipt.'

'Yessir.' The next signal from *Invergarry* indicated that the challenge had been answered correctly. The other vessel was another destroyer of the escort, rejoining: the *Invermore*. She reported her consort believed sunk: the *Aberfeldy* had last been seen at the height of the storm, listed badly and down by the head. She had subsequently been lost to view and had not reappeared. Mason-Goodson expressed no concern at the fate of the lost ship but was pleased at *Invermore* rejoining: she would be able to assist in hauling his command round in due course.

The signalman, on relief from his watch, remarked that it was just as well *Invergarry* hadn't opened fire like the skipper had wanted. 'Daft old fart,' he said witheringly. He said it very much aloud, relieving his feelings, and never mind that the RPO was in the offing, ears a-cockbill. Not even the crusher would want to put him in the rattle, up before the Captain, and have to repeat the charge in full: 'Did call you a daft old fart, sir.'

No metaphorical alarms bells were as yet ringing in the Admiralty or in the headquarters of FOIC Greenock. The carrier and her escort were not due to arrive off the Virginia Capes for some days yet; if they were reported by the US Naval Operating Base at Norfolk as overdue, then there would be concern; but not yet. No one was particularly worried, though there were reservations about the effect of the violence of the weather taken in conjunction with the somewhat vague report from the Officer of the Watch aboard the *Queen Mary*. Reservations, but certainly nothing more. Ships, after all, were built to withstand storms and in the North Atlantic storms were certainly not rare. After another day or two had gone by, *Charger* and her attendant destroyers were pushed to the background of authority's mind. The war at sea was going on, each day, almost each hour, bringing more news, mostly bad, more sinkings of desperately needed merchant vessels as Hitler's surface raiders and U-boat packs decimated the convoys crossing the oceans from Australia and New Zealand, South Africa and UK, to and from the

Mediterranean and the Far East, hauling troop divisions, foodstuffs, guns and munitions, all the muscle of war dependent on keeping the sea lanes open.

So much to be thought about, so many decisions constantly to be made. Even FOIC Greenock was apathetic now, though the Chief of Staff did make a reference to the *Charger*.

'The who?'

'The escort carrier, sir, in mid – '

'Oh, yes, yes.' FOIC stubbed out a cigarette in an overflowing ashtray. 'What's happened to my damn steward, no damn use if he can't keep me supplied with clean ashtrays, what?' He sat back at full arms' stretch from his desk. '*Charger*. What about her? Has there been some word?'

'No, sir, nothing. That's what I was about to say. I don't like it.'

'Oh, she'll be all right, you'll see. Time enough to worry if she fails to be reported from Norfolk.'

'It could be too late by then.'

'What?' The Admiral looked at his wrist-watch. 'Too late –yes, it could be, but I don't think so. You're a worrier, old boy. It doesn't pay, take my word for that. I try not to worry.'

FOIC got to his feet. 'I've an appointment this afternoon, remember. If I'm wanted, contact me at the Turnberry Hotel.' The Chief of Staff nodded: the Admiral was worried about keeping up his handicap and the golf course at Turnberry was a very pleasant one and championship standard at that.

12

'Now is the time,' Mason-Goodson said.

'The time, sir?' Cameron thought there was something extra odd in the Captain's manner. He had uttered suddenly, when Cameron had in fact believed him to be sleeping in his exposed position below the break of the fo'c'sle, sleeping from sheer exhaustion. He had spoken almost with a kind of fervour, an excitement – almost feverishly. He might well be suffering from a fever and if so the doctor should be sent for. But the suggestion was not likely to please Mason-Goodson.

Mason-Goodson spoke again. 'That is what I said, Cameron. Do you dispute it?'

'No, sir – '

'I'm glad to hear that, Cameron, very glad, because I would not like to hear you disputing the word of authority.'

'No, sir.'

'The time, you see, has come to make the turn to port. I am advised that this is so.'

'The conditions haven't improved since – '

'A better judge than you, Cameron, does not appear to agree. I shall turn my ship to port so as to steady her – and save her. Pass the word by semaphore to *Invergarry* and *Invermore*. I shall require the assistance of both of them. *Invergarry* to tow ahead, *Invermore* astern to haul my counter to starboard. Send for the chief bosun's mate. He is to prepare to tow fore and aft.'

The message went to Chief Petty Officer Stoner. Cameron sent also for the PMO.

There was a stir amongst the hands when Stoner passed the order. They didn't like it; things had gone wrong last time and the weather had improved only a very little since then. There was the very real danger of their being pooped if the still high seas dropped down flat on the exposed deck aft of the flight deck. In the old days at any rate ships had been lost by being pooped, their sterns smashed and the water flooding in overwhelmingly to waterlog them and sink them. Also, it was known that the order had come from Mason-Goodson. According to the galley wireless in the form of the signalman and messenger on watch, there had been an oblique reference to God. Also according to the buzz, Lieutenant-Commander Cameron had queried the order.

Chief Petty Officer Malting was aft with the *Charger*'s own PO of the quarterdeck division who would be taking *Invermore*'s towing pendant on the starboard side aft. Malting put a stopper on the moans about Mason-Goodson.

'Captain knows what he's at, don't you worry.' The words were hollow: he didn't believe them himself. Mason-Goodson, by what he'd heard, wasn't in charge. God was. Ben Malting was a God-fearing man right enough, a believer even if he didn't go to church other than when attendance at services aboard were compulsory. God was good and God was great, no question. But was He a seaman, did He fully reckon the dangers of trying to turn a near-helpless ship in such a way as to expose her to pooping?

Maybe; and maybe not. Maybe not enough time to think about about it properly, all those demands constantly going up to Him, what with the Jerries praying as well, praying for victory over the British. God was watch on, stop on, no relief in sight. A very busy life. The *Charger* was just a part of it all, no more than that, whatever she might be to those aboard.

'What the devil are you doing here, PMO?'

'I thought – '

'Then don't. Never *think* – *know*. I've no patience with thinkers, PMO. Meanwhile, you're cluttering up the deck.' Mason-Goodson stared malevolently at MacAllister. 'Who got you to come bothering me?'

'No one, sir. My duty – '

'Balls to your duty, PMO. There's nothing wrong with me except for my damn ankles. They can wait till I have my ship in a safer position – my ship comes first, do you understand?' Mason-Goodson bent to scratch beneath the sea-soaked plaster on his right ankle. 'An itch, but don't you interfere. I've already said, you're cluttering up the deck. So go away.'

'Sir, I – '

'An order, PMO.'

Mason-Goodson's face was formidable. Formidable and, so far as MacAllister was able to judge, sane. MacAllister said as much to Cameron out of the Captain's hearing. 'I've absolutely no reason to query his state of mind. Absolutely none. He appears to know exactly what he's doing.'

'I don't believe it's his own unaided idea, PMO. The . . . visionary angle I suppose you could call it. He's putting the ship at risk – '

'I'm not qualified to pronounce on seamanship, Cameron. Only on medical matters. And I find no medical grounds to interfere. I'm sorry, but there it is.'

No help there. Cameron shrugged and went back for'ard to join the Captain. He would do all he could to save the ship in spite of Mason-Goodson.

Mr Trimby, co-opted by Chatterton to supervise in the tiller flat, watch over the steering engine, had become convinced that he was now facing death. No ship, he believed, could go on taking the constant lurching and bucketing, not for much longer, to say nothing of the undoubted fact that before long the ingress of seawater was going to overcome the now manually operated pumps. She could go suddenly and he along with all the others would be trapped down there in the tiller flat, no time to escape.

In that event, he would be up for judgment any time now. Great danger, imminent death, he found, really concentrated the mind. Eternal life or eternal damnation, that was the choice every man and every woman on earth had. On earth – that was the nub! Once you'd left earth behind, you'd made your choice and you were left with the consequences. Having writ, the moving hand moves on, or words to that effect anyway. You couldn't, in short, scrub out the past. It was there and that was all about it.

That afternoon in Wolverhampton was going to count, no two ways about that, there was a lot in the scriptures, Mr Trimby believed, about adultery. In biblical times adulterers were put to death by stoning, a very nasty end indeed; but on the other hand Jesus had reprimanded the mob when they'd been about to stone a young woman, saying that those without sin should cast the first stone, something like that, or was it glass houses – anyway, the yobs had been made to feel ashamed of themselves and Jesus had forgiven the woman. Mr Trimby, whose knowledge of the Bible was in fact scanty, couldn't remember whether or not it was the first time the young lady had done it.

Mr Trimby's sister-in-law was not the first woman with whom Mr Trimby had done it outside marriage, but the Wolverhampton episode naturally stuck in the mind more firmly on account of their having been caught whilst at it, which hadn't ever been the case in earlier seductions, if you could call them that. It had usually been a financial transaction.

Hong Kong had been the best; or perhaps the Jap ports, now closed to Britain. The Japanese girls had known a thing or two. Also the Siamese. The Orient was much more broadminded than Wolverhampton. . . .

Mr Trimby caught himself up. He had almost shocked himself; he'd been gloating over past misdeeds and that was of course very wrong. Now he realized that he was compounding a felony as might be said, and he closed his eyes in prayer. The prayer was interrupted by a sudden booming sound that seemed to go right through the ship like the knell of doom, and at the same time the carrier gave a very nasty lurch, a sort of twisting motion.

'What was that?' Mason-Goodson twisted his body round to look aft.

He got his answer when a shout came from Cameron in the starboard for'ard walkway. Cameron called down past the lifted end of the flight deck. '*Invermore*, sir – she's been thrown against the port side right aft!'

'Damn clumsiness!' Mason-Goodson fumed. He shouted back, 'Investigate damage and report back at once.'

Cameron was already on his way aft. Looking over the raised starboard side, he saw the destroyer trying to pull clear. The kerfuffle under her counter indicated her engines moving full astern, but she appeared to be making no sternway against the seas that dropped down with immense weight on her quarterdeck, pushing her back against the carrier's plates. Reaching the after deck, Cameron leaned dangerously over the guardrail. Just above the waterline there was a big indentation obviously made by the destroyer's bows, but so far as Cameron could see there was no fracture. As he'd descended from the walkway he'd seen the shipwright making his way below as fast as he could. Cameron followed, making for the engine-room. He contacted the engineer officer. Chatterton was awaiting a report from Tapp, who had joined the shipwright and was sounding round internally. Chatterton wasn't happy, though he reported his engine OK and the screw still not racing.

'I hope Father knows what he's doing,' he said. 'I don't like the feel of the ship.'

Neither did Cameron. He believed she was dying, but knew that no order to abandon ship could be given in current conditions. Lieutenant(E) Tapp came back with the shipwright. Cameron had been right: there was no fracture.

'That having been said,' Tapp added, 'there's further strain on the plates and that means on the seams as well.'

If more welded seams split, the inflow of the water would increase, so much was obvious. Cameron made his way back to the Captain, still seated on his empty whisky case, and reported.

'You're saying the ship's in no extra danger, Cameron, isn't that the case?'

'For now, sir, yes – '

'Then you agree. No extra danger.'

'If the seams go, sir, then the danger will be increased.'

'In your view.'

'Yes, sir.'

'But not in mine.'

'Sir, I – '

'Kindly don't argue with me, Cameron. You're young. You lack experience. You must accept that I know best. I shall continue my attempt to turn my ship to port. I take it *Invermore* is making further attempts to pass the tow?'

'Yes, sir, but – '

'No buts, if you please, Cameron, just see to it that my orders are obeyed, that's all.'

Cameron stood his ground. He said firmly, 'In my opinion, sir, the attempt should be delayed. And I believe you should order all hands up from below. Engine-room, tiller flat . . . it's a trap down there, sir.'

'A trap that must remain,' Mason-Goodson said evenly – almost smiling, Cameron believed. 'For the good of the ship, which will live to fight another day.' He paused, flung water from his eyes as the waves curled overhead and dropped again and again. 'Tell me one thing, Cameron: what would you do that differs from what I'm doing?'

'I've already said, sir – delay the attempt to turn.'

'Yes. And then what? Wait for my ship to break up? Abandon?' Mason-Goodson stared hard at Cameron. There was a look of something like triumph in his eyes now and they glittered with a strange light. 'It's a difficult question,

Cameron, is it not? One that I see *you* are not prepared to answer. Do you understand me?'

Cameron had understood. It was fifty-fifty. Mason-Goodson might be right. There was nothing anyone could do but make a choice between the two alternatives and perhaps one was as likely as the other to be right.

In the meantime, whichever way it went, Cameron knew that the ship was fighting a losing battle. He made his way back aft. *Invermore* had by this time got a heaving line aboard and the hands under Ben Malting were taking it through the fairlead and across to the bitts on the port side. A heavy wire hawser was made fast to the end of the heaving line; the hands sweated and cursed as they tailed onto the wire, heaving it with desperate effort through the sea that swirled across the deck, dragging it inch by inch to the bitts until the eye could be dropped into place and the word given to the destroyer to take up the slack, take the strain of the tow that would swing the stern round and thus assist the for'ard tow to bring the head to port. But again and again the tow slacked off as *Invermore* was taken by the waves behind her and driven back towards the carrier, to fall away again as the stern pull of her engines took effect. Ben Malting, streaming water, shouted to Cameron.

'She's not going to make it, sir! If you ask me, the bloody wire's going to part, going slack at one moment and coming under strain the next, it's not going to go on taking it.'

Malting was right; Cameron had seen that danger for himself. So had the Captain of *Invermore*. Cameron saw him lift a megaphone and heard, faintly, the shout down from the bridge to the cable party on the destroyer's fo'c'sle. It came just too late. As the heavy hawser came once again bar-taut between the two vessels, it started to strand in the *Invermore*'s bullring and then, with terrifying suddenness, it parted. It came back under immense strain in a lethal whiplash movement, flying back over the hands on the carrier's after deck, caught them before they could move out of its flailing path. Two of the seamen were decapitated where they stood, the smashed heads rolling into the scuppers and the bodies dropping in pools of blood that were quickly washed away by the sea. Three other men were caught in the wire coils, screaming in agony as legs and stomachs were crushed as though by some immense and steel-bound boa constrictor. A stranded end of wire had taken another in the throat, which was ripped from one ear to the other. Cameron, partly shielded by what was left of the 4-inch gun-mounting, suffered only the sleeves of his oilskin, duffel-coat and uniform jacket scored right through, only just short of the flesh of his right arm.

'A cack-handed bunch,' was Mason-Goodson's comment when Cameron reported. He was in a flat fury: *Invermore*'s captain had refused point-blank to pass another tow. His own ship was in danger and he saw no prospect of being able to assist the carrier. He gave it as his opinion, unasked, that the whole manoeuvre should be abandoned until the weather was suitable. Mason-Goodson's response was that his refusal would be reported for Admiralty consideration; but in the meantime Mason-Goodson was forced to concede: without a tug aft he would have little hope of success and that was a fact he had to face. He faced it in a storming temper, saying that the commanding officer of the *Invermore* should face Court Martial for cowardice and for causing the deaths and injuries aboard *Charger*: he should never have sent a wire hawser across in the prevailing conditions, at any rate not without a coir spring.

'The idiot in charge aft on my quarterdeck,' Mason-Goodson added, 'is equally culpable. He should have seen to it for himself. Who is he?' The question was directed at Cameron.

'Myself, sir.' This was not strictly true: CPO Malting had been in direct charge.

'Oh. Then it's a pity the wire didn't kill you as well.'

*

Like Cameron, Ben Malting had been lucky, just escaping death. Malting had so often, on that past commission with Cameron, spoken of his family, especially of Bessie and the pub in Queen Street. Cameron knew he had a daughter. He'd never said very much about her but reading between the lines Cameron had formed the impression that she was something of a handful who'd been in need of a father home more often than had been possible for a torpedo-coxswain in time of war. But for chance there might have been no father ever again. Petty Officer Berridge, chief buffer-to-be of the *Veracity* if ever they made it to the Norfolk navy base, was having similar thoughts as he stood by on the fo'c'sle where the hands were currently casting off the tow for'ard, this being no longer required by order of Mason-Goodson. Ben Malting was an old mate; and Berridge had already put his close shave down to Mason-Goodson's rashness. Captain Mason-Goodson may well have had plenty of experience behind him, but in PO Berridge's view he lacked judgment. Young Cameron . . . he may have been foolhardy in attempting the turn to starboard earlier but at least it had been more sensible, Berridge thought, than risking a pooping that had achieved nothing but a number of men lost totally unnecessarily, Ben Malting very nearly among them. If Ben had gone, what would Bessie have done? Go on running the pub all by herself, Berridge supposed. She was capable enough, but that girl of hers wouldn't have been much help.

And what about the rest of them, in Mason-Goodson's hands? Berridge had overheard some of the Captain's statements when Cameron had made his report a short while ago. He'd heard Mason-Goodson say that in his opinion the likely splitting of more welded seams wasn't going to endanger the ship any further. That, Berridge knew, was a proper potty thing to say, so daft that it could only have been said by someone who wasn't thinking straight – was no longer capable of thinking straight.

They had a bloody madman in charge.

It was really a job for the medics.

By now there was a surge of lower-deck opinion against Mason-Goodson. Just about the only support he now had came from those stalwart disciplinarians, the master-at-arms and his regulating petty officer. And even they were keeping their heads down, tending for once to suffer from the disease known as cloth ears. They too had lives to lose. And if there was trouble they looked like being in a minority of two. They would never be able to hold a mob in check, that was obvious. And the mood was now very, very nasty, such that one more spark could set off an explosion. The deaths of the seamen aft had really struck home, had gone very deep.

'They're not *reasoning* any more, Charlie,' Master-at-Arms Horner said. He was finding shelter of a sort at the after end of the hangar, in a small cubby-hole normally in use by the flight deck party when a Fleet Air Arm squadron was embarked.

'Meaning?' the RPO asked.

'Well, meaning this: in actual fact there's nothing the skipper can do, or anybody else either. But they're not seeing that, see. They're out for blood, one way and another. Can't you see that?'

The RPO gave a sudden shiver, and not only from the all-pervading cold and wet. The mere thought of a mutiny was enough to give anyone the willies. The RPO had been a leading stoker in the flagship of the Atlantic Fleet when the men had mutinied at Invergordon, back in the early 1930s. Over a pay grievance, that had been, far from a matter of life and death, but it had been bad enough in its after-effects. A number of promising careers had gone for a burton in that abortive mutiny. Jolly Jack Tar never did win out in the end, not against the perishing might of Admiralty.

The first overt sign was in the form of a deputation to Cameron, who was approached by a leading seaman acting as spokesman.

'Beg pardon, sir.'

'Yes, what is it?'

'If I might just have a word, sir.'

Cameron had sensed what was to come: the man's whole attitude was a giveaway. He was obviously ill at ease, had obviously screwed himself up to something, was equally obviously quite determined to make his point.

Cameron said, 'Go ahead. What's your name?'

'Gossage, sir – '

'All right, Gossage, let's have it.'

'Yessir.' The leading seaman cleared his throat. He was meeting Cameron's eye; Cameron summed him up as a decent man deputed to do a difficult and probably unwelcome job. 'It's the men, sir. All departments, sir.'

'Go on.'

'Yessir. They don't like what's going on, sir. What the Captain's up to.'

Cameron frowned. ' "Up to" is a somewhat unfortunate expression, Gossage.'

'Yessir.' The reply was stolid, obstinate. 'They think he's putting the ship in danger, sir. Putting their lives in danger.'

'Let's get this straight,' Cameron said in a hard tone. 'Are you making a report, or are you stating a case?'

'Stating a case, sir.'

Cameron gave a short laugh. 'Well, that's honest. Are you hostilities-only, Gossage, or long service?'

'Long service, sir.'

'I see. Then you know the ropes.'

'Yes, sir, I do.'

'You know that to represent a complaint on behalf of other persons can be considered an act of mutiny.'

Gossage nodded. 'Yes, sir, I do know that.'

'Then take what I've said as a warning, Gossage. Don't push your luck. The very least that can happen to you is disrating, the loss of your hook and any good-conduct badges.'

'Yes, sir. An' DQS,' Gossage added in reference to the detention quarters in the naval barracks. 'I know all that, sir.'

'So I advise you – '

'It's not advice I'm after, sir. Begging your pardon . . . there's more confidence aboard in you, sir, than in the skipper. We all want you to take command, sir. It's if you don't that there's likely to be trouble. Have the quack – sorry, sir, PMO – take a gander at the skipper and get 'im put on the sick list. That's all, sir. Then there'll be no trouble.'

Gossage stared into Cameron's eyes, his own filled with a sort of pleading, an earnestness that could not summarily be cast aside. Cameron was in a quandary: mutiny was not just about to happen, it seemed, but it was very much on the cards. Did he put Gossage in the report for incipient mutinous conduct, or did he, in effect, give way to threat and approach the PMO?

13

MUTINY WAS the navy's ultimate dread and the punishment was severe: the Articles of War authorized death, though in modern times death was unlikely to be inflicted. The Articles of War had many alternatives and in fact for most naval crimes or misdemeanours the retributive paragraph read 'death or such other punishment as is hereinafter mentioned', the other punishment frequently being no more than stoppage of pay and leave. But historically death was always the price of mutiny. In the old wooden walls, the line-of-battle ships such as Nelson's *Victory*, the Marines had been berthed between the officers and the seamen, their rifles and bayonets ready to preserve the lives of the officers. Mutiny in those days had been a very real prospect. The conditions, the harsh discipline, the frequent floggings when a man was roped to the gratings and lashed with the lead-weighted cat-o'-nine-tails that he had himself constructed for his own torture during the day before the punishment, one hundred and fifty lashes being not unusual . . . such a life had produced reaction, whatever the known consequences. Desperate men had risked a keel-hauling, or a hanging from the main lower topsail yardarm. And even today in the 1940s the old traditions were alive and kicking: the Marines, when carried, were still berthed amidships, still there to act if mutiny should come.

Charger carried no Marines.

The handful of officers could be overwhelmed fast enough. But to subdue those officers would in fact get the lower deck nowhere, unless the officers were prepared to act under duress, under the rifle of some horny-handed able seaman giving the orders. That way would lead to disaster. After a hasty conference with Neil Grey and the master-at-arms, Cameron decided to speak to the lower deck. Without reference to Mason-Goodson.

First, all officers not immediately required in the various parts of the ship were assembled in the after end of the steeply listed hangar. Chatterton came up from the engine-room with Tapp and three more engineer officers, plus Mr Trimby. Briefly Cameron gave them the facts. Lieutenant(E) Tapp looked surly, as though he was in sympathy with the lower deck, but after a look from Chatterton he kept his mouth shut. Mr Trimby, still thinking about death and retribution, was shaking like a leaf and looking sick.

When Cameron had finished, he nodded at the master-at-arms, who raised his voice in a shout to the ship's company, a shout that cut through the booming sound that constantly filled the hangar.

'Right,' he said, and proceeded to give the customary order for all hands to muster, odd though it sounded in the present conditions. 'Clear lower deck, hands to muster in the fore end of the hangar. Quick about it.'

There was some laughter; a man shouted back that they were there already, or didn't he know?

'None of your lip,' Horner said in a harsh tone. The men remained mostly where they were: sitting or lying on the steel deck. Master-at-Arms Horner opened his mouth again; Cameron laid a hand on his arm.

'Leave it, Master,' he said quietly. He'd seen that Leading Seaman Gossage had risen to his feet and was now advising the others to do likewise. No point, he seemed to be saying, in deliberately raising the temperature.

Gossage spoke across the gap to Cameron. 'All here, sir. Those that can be.'

Cameron understood. There had been the deaths that had sparked off the the trouble. There were the sick and injured, under the care of the sick-bay staff. He said, 'Thank you, Gossage.' He raised his voice to the others. 'Come in closer. I want you all to hear clearly what I'm going to say to you. And I'm not going to be too formal about it. There won't be any bullshit today. The matter's too serious for that.' He paused while the men closed in. 'Leading Seaman Gossage has told me how you all feel. I understand those feelings but I'm not going to comment further on that – except to stress that Captain Mason-Goodson still commands this ship and no authority other than the Admiralty itself can alter that fact – '

'What if 'e's gone barmy?' a voice shouted. 'Gone round the bend like? What then, eh? What about the bloody quack?'

Cameron said, 'Allow me to continue. Gossage?'

Gossage understood. He rounded on the men behind him. 'Give the officer a hearing,' he said. 'He's the one we depend on, all right?'

They seemed to accept that. A buzz of conversation that had started up, stopped again. Cameron continued. 'You must all realize that what you're doing is close to mutiny. You all know the risks you're taking – I shan't stress that angle. What I will stress is the utter lunacy of what you're attempting to do. Just think for a moment: how many of you are capable of sailing a ship in our condition – and how many of you are capable of navigating her afterwards, if you should succeed in bringing her through?'

There was a silence, an uneasy one. All the seaman petty officers, under Chief PO Stoner, knowing what was going to happen, had ranged themselves alongside the wardroom officers when Horner had passed the order to clear lower deck. That symbolic movement deprived the would-be mutineers of virtually all the experienced men. Cameron waited a moment then said, 'You'd not have a snowflake in hell's chance and you know it. You want to get home to UK – don't you?'

There was another silence; then a voice called out, 'We won't get anywhere under the skipper. It's you we want. You'll do what we want, mate, with a rifle in your bloody backside!'

Which was precisely what Cameron had foreseen as the most likely outcome if the mutiny should take place. There would not in fact be rifles available to the lower deck; the rifles were customarily locked in racks under the charge of the keyboard sentry, and were issued only in special circumstances such as the formation of landing or boarding parties – not in any case a likely role for an aircraft-carrier. Those rifles were still in the racks outside the Captain's quarters and before speaking to the lower deck Cameron had placed an armed petty officer on the racks. The most likely weapons in fact would be the seamen's knives and perhaps sawn-off metal chair legs and so on from the wardroom and POS' mess, plus spanners and crowbars and other heavy metal objects from the engineers' store. What Cameron wished at all costs to avoid was the provocation of arming the officers from the rifle racks. In any case it was unlikely anyone would get through what would be a mob, in order to bring them down. . . .

There was now a new dimension: an actual threat had been uttered. At Cameron's side, Master-at-Arms Horner shifted uneasily from one foot to another and whistled through his teeth. He guessed that Cameron was out of his depth now. He offered unasked advice. 'If I was you, sir, I'd crack down hard. It's now or never in my opinion.'

'What the hell do I crack down with?'

Horner shrugged, hugging his clipboard to his chest. He'd given his opinion, the rest wasn't up to him. Cameron carried the two-and-half gold stripes of a lieutenant-commander: those gave him the responsibility. Horner sucked at his teeth: the RNVR, the Wavy Navy as they called them, were all very well; but there were situations they'd never been trained to deal with, and this was one. Horner himself believed in toughness. You had to show you were harder than the rank-and-file or they would suss it out soon enough and then you were done for. Had Horner been in charge he would have conducted the speechifying from the walkway over the hangar, leading from the Captain's lobby where the rifles were. Any trouble then, and he'd have had the whip hand, fully prepared to fire down on the ringleaders. Knock those buggers off and the rest would cave in – stood to reason, did that. But he knew Cameron would never do that. Too soft.

There was a movement now amongst the ratings. Gossage was being pushed into the background, pushed aside as the others crowded closer towards the small group of officers. Horner spoke from the side of his mouth: 'Watch it, sir.'

Cameron, with Neil Grey at his side, stood his ground. He believed that actual blows would not be struck. The moment that happened, the men would have mutinied and there would be no going back. He believed that they would not commit themselves just yet. There would still be time for talking, for trying to drive into their minds the folly they were about to commit, a folly that could end in the ship being in a worse position than ever. He called on them to stand back, to take time to consider what they were about to do, how irrevocable would be the next act. He reminded them that two of the destroyer escort were still in company and that the commanding officers might smell a rat. But even as he spoke the words he realized their intrinsic emptiness: in the sea that was still running, neither of the destroyers would be able to put an armed party aboard the carrier.

As before it was Gossage who stilled the derisive laughter that came from the hands. Then, once again the clear leader, he turned to Cameron.

'You can put a stopper on it easily enough, sir. Just get a medical report from the doctor, sir. That's all. After that, the lads'll be right behind you. All of them. Give it a thought, sir. For all our sakes.'

Cameron found the PMO beside him. He asked in a low voice, 'What do you think, PMO?'

'Mason-Goodson is not insane, Cameron. It would be quite wrong of me to say anything other than that.'

'But if the alternative is – '

'There is my Hippocratic oath, my dear chap.'

There was finality in MacAllister's tone. That avenue, if ever it had existed, was now closed. It seemed to be an impasse and time had almost run out. The men's mood was growing visibly harder, their patience evaporating. Acts of insubordination carried their own momentum, and when you had got away with a little you wanted more. There was real hostility in the air now; Cameron was the one they wanted to see them through, but Cameron was still one of the afterguard and by that token the enemy who was refusing, obstinately, to concede.

Back in the Clyde area fresh reports had come into the office of FOIC Greenock: a destroyer of the Clyde Escort Force, returning to base with a convoy which she had brought in from forty west, broke wireless silence on passing inwards of Ailsa Craig. South and east of Greenland's Cape Farewell survivors had been picked up. These survivors, found just about alive in a Carley float, a miracle if ever there was one in such seas, had not come under any enemy attack. The story came out piecemeal from exhausted men. Their ship had been overcome by the mountainous seas, broaching to when a fault had developed in the steering, and she had gone down with almost all her ship's company. The men, three of them, in the Carley float were the only known survivors. Their ship had been a destroyer from the flotilla acting as escort to the *Charger*.

When the signal was handed to the Flag Officer in Charge he demanded a full report, to be made in person by the commanding officer of the incoming destroyer immediately after entry to the anchorage.

When this report was made some two hours later, FOIC was given the survivors' story: the storm in mid-Atlantic had overwhelmed the carrier and her escort, and *Charger* had last

147

been seen lying broadside to the wind and sea and listed heavily.

'That report from the *Queen Mary*,' the Admiral said to his Chief of Staff.

'Exactly, sir.'

'Action this minute – and a prayer it won't be too late! Tugs to leave the Clyde soonest possible. See to that right away.'

'The Admiralty – '

'I'll deal with the Admiralty.' FOIC picked up his security line to the Operations Room in London. The Chief of Staff took up another telephone and passed the orders to despatch the ocean-going rescue tugs to an approximate position as estimated by the CO of the recently arrived destroyer. Only one tug, it appeared, had steam at immediate notice; a second tug would leave Londonderry to rendezvous with the one from the Clyde off Malin Head outside Lough Swilly.

These movements were reported to the Admiralty. In the Operations Room ratings of the WRNS shifted counters on the big wall map. Once again the room was filled with the Prime Ministerial cigar smoke: Winston Churchill always followed the naval movements, when he was able to be present, most keenly. This time he was critical.

'It would appear,' he said heavily, 'that much time has been lost. Perhaps too much time. Whose fault is that, may I ask?' He was staring at the Duty Captain.

'No one's fault, sir. We're stuck with what facilities are available. There's a shortage of rescue tugs in all commands.'

'A shortage of brains too, I fancy,' the Prime Minister growled. 'Not to mention common humanity . . . however, I take your point about shortages. I can assure you, Captain, that words will be said in certain quarters that will listen – and act, or have me to reckon with afterwards.'

Which would be of no current help to the *Charger*, the Duty Captain reflected, wondering why it always took what seemed to be a tragedy to make people think about the provision of adequate back-up facilities for those doing the actual fighting out at sea whether it be against the enemy or against the weather. For those in peril on the sea. . . .

Aboard the carrier there had been a totally unexpected diversion.

As the men closed further in towards the officers and the tension mounted there came a shout from the fore end of the hangar, a shout from Stripey Haslam.

'Lootenant-Commander Cameron, sir – Captain wants you.'

Cameron spoke to the men confronting him. 'You heard that. Let me through.'

There was no movement. Cameron said, 'That's an order. If you want a mutiny, the way to start is to disobey that order.'

There was still no movement. Cameron outfaced them. Master-at-Arms Horner came up beside him, his face like a rock. Cameron took a pace forward, and the man nearest him stepped back a pace. No one wished to be the first actually to disobey an order, the first to perform an act of mutiny. Cameron moved on another pace and there was a sideways movement. The mob parted to give the officer free passage. Cameron said, 'Thank you. When I've seen the Captain, I may have more to say to you.'

Shoulder to shoulder he and the master-at-arms moved on through. The tension was building close to breaking point, and the overall hostility to authority was almost tangible, as was the ambiance of fear – fear of what was happening to the ship and fear, too, of what the next move was going to be. Cameron believed that not all the men would be found willing to go to the extreme length of mutiny at sea in time of war. It would be a good thing for that fear to sink in deep before the situation went right beyond the point of no return.

Stripey Haslam was waiting. Cameron asked, 'Where's the Captain, Haslam?'

'Still where 'e was, sir. I'd stayed on the fo'c'sle, sir, during the muster, not wanting to blot me copybook, like. Captain, 'e sent me for you, sir.'

149

'Does he know what's going on here in the hangar?'

Stripey Haslam had a bewildered look. He said, 'I don't reckon 'e does, sir, no. I don't reckon . . . Captain's acting odd, sir. More odd, like, than before, sir.'

A matter, at last, for the PMO? Cameron made his way to the Captain's position beneath the break of the fo'c'sle, followed by MAA Horner and Stripey Haslam.

14

ACROSS THE North Atlantic in Wolverhampton matters were coming to the boil. The aggrieved Mrs Trimby had brooded and brooded on what she had seen and the enormity of it all had taken permanent root. She simply could not go on living with Alf, dusting round the parlour where the act had taken place, seeing it again every time she straightened the antimacassars. And in the end, largely on account of financial matters, even her mother had come to see a divorce as the best answer. The only one really: errant husbands had to be brought to book.

The solicitor, who was paid to be sympathetic, agreed. 'Oh, quite,' he said in his fusty office. 'Very right and proper, Mrs Trimby. We all know what sailors are.' He didn't, but he had heard about loose morals among the seafaring community, of which there were in fact not many in Wolverhampton. Mr Benton of Benton, Son and Makepeace knew all about wives in every port, that sort of thing, and brothels abounding throughout the Empire. This, however, was different since it involved a sister-in-law.

'Tell me the facts, Mrs Trimby. In full. Leave nothing out.'

She did so. 'Such a scene I never did see,' she declared.

'I should think not indeed. Have the facts been disputed? Was there, shall we say, any denial? From either party?'

'Well, there couldn't be, could there?' Mrs Trimby stared

back at Mr Benton in astonishment. 'I see it with my own eyes, the lot. How could they deny it, eh?'

Mr Benton shrugged. 'You'd be surprised,' he said vaguely. 'However, I shall take it that the facts are not in dispute. I foresee little difficulty in all the circumstances. Of course, you realize your sister will be quoted as the co-respondent. Somewhat . . . disagreeable, that. You've considered that, of course?'

'Well, what else?' Mrs Trimby demanded, her voice shrill. 'Janet was the one what he was doing it with, wasn't she?'

'Of course, yes.' Mr Benton was embarrassed; there had been no need to be quite so explicit. 'Now – '

'Now about the money,' Mrs Trimby interrupted. 'The 'ouse and all. I got to have a home. And income.'

'That will be – '

'No good 'im thinking he can go off to sea all nice and comfortable aboard a ship and get away with leaving me penniless.'

'No, quite. I understand fully. Sailors do tend, I think, to believe they can get away with – with – '

'Adultery. Yes. I'm going to take 'im for 'is last ha'penny, see if I don't,' Mrs Trimby said. When the business had been concluded, or at any rate advanced as far as was possible at this early stage, Mrs Trimby left the offices of Benton, Son and Makepeace and caught the bus back to her mother's house. She made her report and the two ladies went out for a celebratory tea, the wheels being now in motion, the decision made. After their tea, Mrs Trimby suggested the pictures. They paid their one-and-sixes and saw Noel Coward in *In Which We Serve*, all about the navy. Blood and thunder and a lot of rough sea. Mrs Trimby's mother hoped vengefully that her errant son-in-law was just like the sailors in the film, facing fearful odds.

Captain Mason-Goodson was leaning back from the whisky case, against the guardrail. He said nothing when Cameron approached, but he seemed to be staring straight into

Cameron's eyes. Cameron said formally, 'You wished to see me, sir.'

There was no answer: the stare remained fixed. Then, suddenly, Mason-Goodson's body slid sideways in a flopping motion and fell to the deck, the water coming over the fo'c'sle surging around him. Cameron, bending, felt for the heart. Mason-Goodson was alive. With the assistance of MAA Horner and Stripey Haslam, he was carried at once into the the shelter of the hangar.

There was only one verdict and MacAllister gave it: Mason-Goodson had suffered a stroke.

Now the feeling throughout the ship was different: a jonah had been removed. Mason-Goodson was alive but he was no longer in command. There had been no need even for Cameron to make an announcement. The lower deck had seen for itself. Mutiny had been averted by a hair's breadth, by a miracle. God was on their side and they would come through: this thought was in very many minds and none of them saw it as in any way incongruous that God should figure in their thoughts just as He had figured in Mason-Goodson's. With God's help and Lieutenant-Commander Cameron in command, they were going to make it to the Virginia Capes.

Once Mason-Goodson had been delivered into medical hands, Cameron had gone with Grey to the starboard for'ard walkway and had tried to make an assessment of the weather.

'Still moderating,' Grey said. 'But slowly.'

'Too damn slowly, Number One. I'm going to leave it a little longer all the same.'

'Risky.'

Cameron glaced sideways. 'Too risky?' he asked.

Grey nodded. 'I believe so. I believe she'll go if we don't correct her list – and take the weight of the sea off her.'

'It's a risk to do that, too. We've already seen – '

Grey interrupted firmly. 'It's a lesser risk. I believe we have to make the attempt before it's too late.'

Cameron weighed things up in his mind. Grey had

undergone a long apprenticeship in the merchant ships before winning his Second Mate's, then his Mate's, and finally his Master's certificates. And many more years in blue-water ships since then. He would be in a better position than Cameron to judge when a ship had had enough, was weary and waiting to go. So many men would go with her if he, Cameron, failed to respond to the voice of experience.

'Right,' he said crisply. 'Make to *Invergarry* and *Invermore*, I intend to resume my turn to port.'

'Aye, aye, sir,' Grey said. He passed the message to the signalman who had accompanied them to the walkway. The message was passed by semaphore and the word went to Chief PO Stoner.

The main fury of the storm had now passed easterly and the sea conditions were atrocious off the Bloody Foreland at the north-eastern tip of County Donegal and some way out towards forty degrees west longitude, though by now falling short of that spot on the chart where the convoy escorts from Scapa Flow or Londonderry or the Clyde took over from the escorts out of Halifax, Nova Scotia. The two ocean-going rescue tugs with their heavy towing gear, having made the rendezvous off Malin Head, butted their stems into the Atlantic rollers, throwing back solid water over their fo'c'sles and bridges as they made the best speed possible towards the estimated position of the carrier lying at the sea's mercy.

A needle in a haystack was the opinion of both the tugs' masters. A ship, any ship, was a small enough object in the vastness of any of the world's oceans. Both tugs would of course be using their radar and that would give them some further scope, but even that would be of little help. If the carrier could transmit homing signals all would have been well; but she would doubtless maintain wireless silence to the end.

And there was the enemy to think about: the moment the weather became suitable, Goering would be sending out his strike planes to harass the convoys in the Western

Approaches, and the U-boat packs, currently deep down beneath the water and the weather, would come again to periscope depth ready to loose off their torpedoes at anything that came within their range.

One enemy would be exchanged for another.

Mr Trimby was back in the tiller flat, watching over the steering engine's restoration to working capacity; in the meantime the hands were hauling the rudderhead over, this time to hard-a-starboard so that the rudder-blade turned to port to assist the turn away from the weight of the sea. There was still the danger of being pooped and amongst the first to be pooped would be Mr Trimby. They always said that a drowning man saw his whole life pass before his eyes in the last few seconds of life, although Mr Trimby wondered how the hell anyone could say this unless he'd drowned himself, in which case he would no longer be there to tell the tale. And although Mr Trimby wasn't exactly drowning yet, he was suffering the symptoms. Or some of them. For the purposes of the whole-life-before-your-eyes theory, Mr Trimby's life was beginning on that fateful afternoon in Wolverhampton.

He was sorry.

He was desperately sorry, wondering for the thousandth time how he'd ever come to be so daft. Other arrangements could have been made; he could – should – have met his sister-in-law somewhere else, somewhere safer, like an air raid shelter when there wasn't a raid on, or a hotel room, or even the garden shed. To do it in the front parlour . . . he must have had a brainstorm, like Mason-Goodson, only different. Talk about lunacy! Or talk about sudden urges that couldn't be denied. And that, of course, was it: he'd been seized by a feeling out of his control, and so had Janet. Not their fault – not really. Passion. There were some things you couldn't not do, but try putting that one across to Maud or her bloody mother.

Watching the engine-room ratings working on the steering engine, watching Ben Malting sweating with the hands on the pulley-hauley at the rudderhead, surging about with the terrible motion of the ship, waiting for death, Mr Trimby conducted an honest search of his mind, his motives and his regrets.

Sorry but glad.

That was it. Or glad but sorry, since the glad part had come first. He'd *enjoyed* it at the time. He had to admit that, since God would know he had anyway, God from whom nothing at all was hid. God would have seen the whole thing, of course He would, and would have divined what was in the minds of the participants. In a curious sort of way Mr Trimby was seeing it as if from above, as though watching it (like God) without actually taking part, which could mean that he was dead already, but he didn't think he was because he could hear the words coming from the gang on the rudderhead tackle and they were not the words you'd expect to hear in the afterlife.

Anyway, he was sorry now. He truly repented. It had all caused so much bother, such a simple little act blown out of all proportion.

He didn't want to be divorced. Maud was difficult, true, but she was better than no wife at all. Try coming back on leave, Mr Trimby thought bitterly, with no one to cook, clean and sew on buttons, mend socks, do the shopping . . . it just wasn't on. And home was home. The house was his, his castle. Mortgaged, yes, but in his name. The Law, however, wouldn't take any account of that, he'd bet his last farthing. They'd have it off him, give half at least to Maud, which would mean selling up.

Leaving him homeless, the buggers. Bailiffs in, probably, nicking the lot.

If he came through this lot, that was. What a prospect, being saved only to face a wrecked life! He was still not keen on starting again with Janet – some start, with no house and alimony payable the rest of his life to Maud, with his mother-in-law probably living on it as well. Janet had been a momentary aberration, an expensive one.

Mr Trimby explained all this to God as best he could, hoping to impress.

His explanations were interrupted by a shout from an engine-room artificer working on the steering engine.

It had come back to life. Perhaps that was an omen. Mr Trimby went himself, post-haste, to report to Lieutenant-Commander Cameron. Anywhere up top was safer than remaining in the tiller flat. Climbing the ladders, he tried to have positive thoughts rather than negative ones. The prospects of coming through were brighter now. And maybe Maud wouldn't go for a divorce at all. She might be sensible and forgive him. She had as much to lose as he had. Nobody else would want to marry her.

The destroyers were buttoned on fore and aft. No more mishaps. When everything was in position and all ropes and wires were being closely watched, Cameron passed the word to *Invergarry* and her consort and the slack of the towing pendants was taken up slowly. *Charger*'s engine was put to slow ahead, with Chatterton back on the starting platform. In the tiller flat, Ben Malting, wiping sweat from his eyes, saw the tackle cast off from the rudder-head and the steering engine connected up to hold the rudder hard over as before.

He watched the gyro repeater, which was still in action.

'She's coming round,' he said.

He remembered having said that before, and on that occasion he'd spoken too soon. Subsequently, everything had gone wrong. But this time the swing seemed to keep up. Very, very slowly the ship's head was coming round, maintaining the swing to port. There was a nasty moment when a sea – a sea that was at last beginning to become a following, instead of a broadside, one – took the after part of the ship with smashing force, sending her stern down deep and then, as it passed beneath the double bottoms, lifting and twisting the hull so that everyone in the tiller flat was thrown off balance to skid and flounder around in the slop of water on the deck plating. But then she steadied up.

'We're doing it,' Malting said, his voice breaking with sheer relief. *'We're bloody doing it!'*

The swing continued. The ship began to ride easier, the list remaining but the up-and-down motion brought about by the action of the beam sea was going, to be replaced by a fore-and-aft motion that, to any seaman, meant the possibility of salvation was within their grasp.

From the walkway Cameron watched, scarcely daring to hope, to believe what he was seeing as the bows swung on to port. The destroyer aft had already been cast off so as to allow her to find her own safety and she was steaming ahead fast to keep well clear of the carrier, which was now under her own power and able to steer by direct movement of the steering engine.

Cameron used a megaphone to shout down to the fo'c'sle.

'Stand by to cast off *Invergarry*.' He turned to the signalman standing behind him. 'Make to *Invergarry*, cast off when ready and stand clear.'

Neil Grey was smiling. He said, 'Congratulations. That was very nicely done.'

Cameron grinned. 'Coming from the RNR, that means something.' He was well aware that he couldn't have done it on his own. 'But we're not out of the wood yet, Number One. First job now is to correct the list.'

Grey nodded. 'I'll put the hands onto clearing the debris from the hangar right away. When that's done, we'll be able to trim her properly.' He paused. 'She's riding . . . not well, but not too badly. With a following sea, and with the weather said to be moderating – '

'Said to be.'

'It will,' Grey said with assurance. 'On past experience, this won't go on much longer. A lot of weight's gone out of it already, we know that.'

Cameron nodded: he seemed to have something else on his mind, Grey thought. Glancing at Cameron he said, 'If all continues well, sir, we should make the Bloody Foreland within two or three days at most.'

'The Bloody Foreland?'

'That'll be our landfall. If the Jerries don't get us.'

Cameron gave a short laugh. 'My dear old chap . . . we're not going that way. Our orders, unless and until they're negatived, are for the Virginia Capes. We have a frigate to pick up – remember?'

The word went quickly round the ship that Cameron wasn't heading for home after all – most of the ship's company had assumed he would, with the ship in her current state. That she would have to go into dockyard hands for a lengthy refit was obvious and there had been that strong hope that they would all be in for a spot of leave.

'Survivors' leave,' Stripey Haslam said. 'Or as good as! We were bloody near in the drink, eh?'

But, of course, she could just as easily be refitted as originally intended in the USA. Plenty of British warships had been refitted across the pond, since America had come into the war following the tragedy of Pearl Harbor. So there were compensations. They could have a good time in America; the Yanks were very hospitable and their dames looked good, anyway as portrayed by Hollywood. Big breasts and that.

Some concern was expressed that there would be difficulty in making another turn, this time to take the ship back across the wind and sea with once again the danger that she might broach to. But it was unlikely that Cameron would attempt this until the weather conditions were absolutely right. And by the time the hangar had been cleared of the debris from the wrecked aircraft, and the trim properly adjusted by the engineers and shipwrights, she would ride a whole lot easier and safer.

All hands were piped by the bosun's mates to muster for the business of clearing up the hangar, and parties were detailed to work under the petty officers and leading hands. The tangle of bodywork and aero engines and propellers was shifted onto the aircraft lifts, after a dummy run to make sure the electrics

159

worked. The lifts conveyed the rubble to the flight deck where it was dumped over the side.

Life was a lot easier. With her two remaining escorts steaming ahead on either bow, the carrier continued on an easterly course towards the Northern Irish coast until such time as Cameron was ready to risk the turn.

As the ship steadied and the decks resumed their normal angle, life came back below. The pumps, now repaired, at least temporarily, sucked the water out of her and the drying-out process began. In the sick bay the two doctors and their sick-berth attendants coped with the injuries and the effects of long-sustained cold and wet. With all the ship's executive officers gone, there were empty cabins with bunks available for the worst cases. In one of them lay Mason-Goodson: he was, according to the PMO, better off as close as possible to medical aid rather than in his own quarters immediately below the lifted end of the flight deck. Those quarters were in any case a fair shambles, for water had penetrated after the lifting of the flight deck.

Leaving the ship in Neil Grey's hands, Cameron went down with the PMO to see Mason-Goodson.

There was life there yet, but by the look of him only just.

'Prognosis?' Cameron asked.

The PMO shrugged. 'Bad. I doubt if he'll last more than a day or so. On the other hand, you never know.'

'And if he recovers, what then?'

Again the PMO shrugged. 'That's imponderable, too. Good recoveries can be made, but he's had a very massive stroke, so I'd say he'd be left helpless both physically and mentally.'

'A vegetable?'

'Yes.'

Cameron's own father had died of a stroke; Cameron had felt only relief that he had not come through to face life as a vegetable, wholly dependent on other people for his every function. Death had to be better than that. There was something terrible about the sight of a man who had commanded ships lying there so helpless, a parody of his former self, all the fires going out even though life clung on.

'Has he a family?' Cameron asked.

'A wife. No children.'

Either way bad news would be reaching the wife once the ship was back in communication with the outside world. Cameron turned away, wondering what, if anything, was going through Mason-Goodson's mind. To be deeply unconscious might well be like having some appalling nightmare, the thoughts going round and round to no effect until waking brought an end to it. Or death . . . Mason-Goodson could be worrying about his ship, or about his wife. Wanting perhaps to ask questions, but unable to formulate them. There was nothing anyone could do about that. Cameron could only hope that his own actions in opposing Mason-Goodson had not been in some degree responsible for the stroke.

He climbed back to the walkway and joined his first lieutenant. Quite suddenly, there was a definite change in the weather. A patch of blue sky appeared to the west, and this extended over the next half-hour. The sea still ran high in the aftermath of the gale but the wind itself had dropped and was dropping further.

'If this goes on,' Cameron said, 'we'll make the turn westerly.'

'When the sea goes down more,' Grey said. 'We have to bear in mind that bloody fixed sail of ours.'

In the middle watch that night, word reached Cameron that Mason-Goodson had died. The word was brought by the surgeon lieutenant. Cameron said he would make the necessary disposal arrangements next morning. The body would be committed to the sea in the proper service manner, with a guard in attendance. He would have a word with Chief Petty Officer Stoner about that. The guard would be paraded at the after end of the flight deck, with gaiters and sidearms, and there would be a piping party as Mason-Goodson went over his ship's side for the last time, from the gundeck aft while the engine lay stopped. He had, after all, been the Captain.

In the early hours of the morning watch, the four to eight, with the first faint flickers of a brighter dawn already lightening the sky in the east, the reports of better weather over the North Atlantic, over the homeward and outward-bound convoy routes that kept embattled Britain supplied with the essentials of war from the United States, reached the German air command in Berlin. Reichsmarschal Goering was informed personally, being woken from the bed in which, according to popular Allied legend, he slept in pyjamas that carried his full set of medals. The fat Reichsmarschal had been upset and irate on account of the weather over the last week or so, weather that had inhibited his so powerful air armadas whose God-given task it was to obliterate Britain and the ships steaming on her vital supply routes.

Within minutes of the Reichsmarschal being woken, the orders were going out to the commands concerned. By the time the morning watch aboard the carrier was half over, the Junkers 88s were leaving their airfields in occupied Norway and heading out across the seas between the Shetlands and Iceland.

15

THE RADAR warning system in the north of Scotland had been largely put out of action in an earlier raid and was not as yet back to full function; and the JU 88s got through the broken screen, heading out unremarked into the North Atlantic. The first vessels to come under attack were the ocean-going rescue tugs, pushing at their maximum speed through the still-disturbed water and using their radar in an attempt to pick up the carrier.

They had no chance: they used their pop-gun ack-ack armament courageously but ineffectively as the JU 88s made their runs, sweeping the tugs' decks and wheelhouses with cannon and machine-gun fire before dropping their bomb loads. The tugs disintegrated beneath fire and flame, going down and leaving no survivors. Before the end came, urgent signals had been made by W/T. With the enemy at hand, there was no point in maintaining wireless silence.

The gaitered and sidearmed guard was paraded under the *Charger*'s chief gunner's mate. Mason-Goodson's body, sewn into its canvas shroud, was borne to the after deck where a plank had been rigged across the bulwarks beside the shattered 4-inch guns. The body, covered with a White Ensign taken down temporarily from the ensign staff at the after end of the flight deck – the whole of the flag and bunting stock had been lost when the flag locker had gone over the

163

side with the bridge superstructure – was placed on the plank with two seamen at the inboard end, ready to tilt when the order came. The engine had been stopped, and the carrier lay still, as silent as was any ship at sea when lying stopped.

Cameron was to read the short, simple service. With him were all the remaining officers except for a sub-lieutenant of the *Veracity* draft who was on watch in the fore end of the starboard walkway. Mr Trimby had come up from the engine-room where he had continued to help out, activity being a sight better than wondering what was going on in Wolverhampton in his absence. He didn't think much about the deceased; Mason-Goodson had never so much as spoken to him. Whilst waiting for Cameron to start reading from a prayer book, Mr Trimby, with nothing else to do at the moment, thought about his troubles. . . .

As to the Captain, there had been mixed comment on the ship. Mason-Goodson's personality had not endeared him but death was death, all said and done.

'It's the missus. . . .'

'Old bastard. Maybe she'll be glad.'

'Won't get much of a welcome up aloft, eh?' There was a snigger. 'Put God in 'is place more'n likely. Or try to.'

'You don't talk ill o' the dead, matey.' This was Stripey Haslam, who had helped carry the Captain into the comparative shelter of the hangar and had been sorry to see the mighty fallen so low. Mason-Goodson may have been a bit of an old sod but he'd been a captain RN and to Stripey that meant something that wasn't easy to put across to what was largely a hostilities-only complement. Them rookies, as Stripey thought of them, just simply didn't understand. They didn't understand the sheer *majesty* of the captain of a ship, the autocracy, the remoteness, the sheer power of any ship's captain, the power of life and death almost. Aboard his ship, the Captain was indeed what Mason-Goodson appeared to believe: God. The Captain could do no wrong. To the uninitiated, however, until they learned different, the Captain was just a bloke with one more gold ring than the

Commander, the bloke who ultimately bossed them, just like the boss ashore, who was usually equally remote and puffed up about it.

Not to Stripey Haslam, who remembered what he thought of as the old navy, the pre-war navy, where officers wore starched collars and cuffs, and you didn't speak to them until they spoke to you, and when they did you stood rigid at attention and then jumped to it at the double. The Captain never spoke to you, of course, except at Defaulters where he pronounced sentence on miscreants who'd overstayed their leave, or returned aboard drunk, or been slow to obey an order, or had socked a PO on the nose. . . .

Cameron, when all was ready, began the service.

'Forasmuch as it hath pleased Almighty God of his great mercy to take unto himself the soul of our dear brother here departed; we therefore commit his body to the deep. . . .' He paused, nodded at the two seamen standing by to tilt the plank. They plank came up a little and as it did so there was a shout from the round-down at the after end of the flight deck.

Cameron looked up.

'From the Officer of the Watch, sir – JU 88s coming in, bearing due east, sir!'

Cameron closed his prayer book with a snap. 'Belay the committal,' he ordered. As the plank was tilted back the other way and Mason-Goodson's body was lowered back inboard, he went fast for the sound-powered telephone to the engine-room.

'Engine to full ahead,' he ordered. 'Aircraft coming in, chief!'

He went fast for the flight deck and the walkway. As he went the bosun's mate was already piping over the Tannoy, sending the ship's company to action stations. Men began pounding the ladders through the ship, the ack-ack gunnery rates going at the double to their guns along the walkways. Below on the starting platform Chatterton watched his dials and gauges as steam was fed from the boilers to turn the great shaft that ran through to the screw. Chatterton didn't think they would have much hope; the 4-inch armament was non-existent and the 40mm guns would have suffered the effect of seawater, and although they'd been stripped down subsequently by the gunner's party they were probably likely to pack up at short notice. They didn't carry much punch in any case.

'Thank God for the destroyers,' he said. 'Our last bloody hope!'

As Chatterton had forecast, the carrier's light ack-ack armament was virtually useless. Despite the earlier efforts of the gunner's party, half of them, it seemed, suffered misfires. The two destroyers put up a good defence, however; the JU 88s – the 'A' version adapted to carry torpedoes – coming in low on a strafing run, didn't have it all their own way. One was shot down within the first couple of minutes, ditching in the still-disturbed sea, and vanishing beneath the waves as the crew tried to struggle clear of the wreckage. But plenty of damage was done to the ships as they manoeuvred desperately to throw off the determined attack. Pieces of metal flew as aboard the carrier the ack-ack armament was taken by cannon fire, and there were heavy casualties. Helm orders went in a constant stream to the men in the tiller flat, men praying that the steering engine wouldn't pack up again and send them back to pulley-hauley. Cameron was finding his view badly restricted by the lifted end of the flight deck, and in order to find a better and more commanding position he doubled aft of the jagged lift of the deck and then left the walkway for the flight deck itself. As he did so one of the attackers, coming in low across the carrier, loosed off a stream of machine-gun fire. Cameron was hit in the right forearm and as he dodged back into the shelter of the walkway he saw Neil Grey stagger and fall overboard. Then another of the Junkers came in from aft, firing down into the port walkway, a stream of fire that effectively silenced what remained of the port-side armament.

That appeared to be the end of the low-level attack. The JUS peeled away, beginning to climb now. The worst, as Cameron knew, was yet to come. The JUs were about to go into their bombing runs.

Within minutes, that was what happened. Those aboard the ships, staring upwards, saw the bomb doors open as one by one the attackers came in again, saw the egg-shaped death dropping clear down upon them.

Cameron did his best to throw off the aim, altering course to port and starboard and back again, as fast as the urgent orders could reach the tiller flat.

Then the bombs began to explode. Some of them hit the sea more or less harmlessly, though a near miss on the *Invergarry*'s starboard bow plating rocked her badly and caused casualties to the crews of her fo'c'sle-mounted guns as splinters flew behind the gunshield. And a moment later another heavy bomb took the quarterdeck of the *Invermore* with devastating results: the depth charges in the racks and throwers went up, blowing away the whole of the after part of the ship, opening her up below the waterline and turning the sea astern of her red with blood beneath a huge pall of smoke and flame. She didn't go straight down; somewhere, a bulkhead was holding yet. But shortly after this another well-placed bomb took her bridge superstructure and the last Cameron saw of her was a smoking, flaming wreck, drifting helplessly, no longer under command, with the survivors jumping from the fo'c'sle plating as the bows came up in her final dive, stern first, beneath the turbulent sea.

Then, quite suddenly, the attack seemed to break off.

Cameron found Ben Malting by his side. Malting was bleeding from a deep gash in his cheek, a gash of which he seemed unaware. He said breathlessly, 'Only three forty-millimetres still in action, sir. I wonder what them buggers are up to now.' He referred to the Junkers 88s, which had withdrawn in formation to the west. 'I bet they won't be leaving us alone, sir.'

'Right. The next thing'll be a torpedo run.' Cameron laid a hand on Malting's shoulder. 'Steering by tiller flat . . . that's no good for manoeuvring. Too slow to answer.'

Malting nodded: he knew the score, knew that the best defence against torpedo attack was to turn the ship towards the oncoming tin-fish, usually made visible by their trails as they approached at around forty knots, make the ship as small a target as possible by meeting them bows on and hope, by fast and tricky helm movements, to avoid them, leaving them to pass harmlessly down the ship's side. This time, there would be little hope of that. Some, but not much; and in the next moment even that small hope was dashed.

A messenger was seen, doubling along the flight deck. In a shaking voice he called out, 'From the tiller flat, sir. Steering engine's packed up again, sir.'

Cameron's heart sank. 'So it's back to pulley-hauley?'

'Yes, sir. They're working on it now, sir.'

Cameron gave an absent nod. There would be no time for anybody to do much good, the aircraft were already turning back towards the carrier and the one remaining destroyer. Cameron said, 'This is it, Malting. There's only one order left to give now.'

'Abandon, sir?'

'Yes. Use the Tannoy. All hands up from below, abandon ship. Swing out all boats and rafts.'

Cameron reached out his hand; Ben Malting took it in a firm grip. 'Never mind, sir. Did your best, you did, and all of us knows that. Now we just hope we make it back to Pompey. One way or another.' Then he turned away to pass the order to abandon. Cameron knew Ben Malting was thinking of his wife, probably worrying about the daughter. Wives and families were always what filled seamen's thoughts during the long absences and when a man came face to face with the prospect of death within perhaps minutes all the things done that should not have been done, and all the things not done that should have been done – they could all come to mind in a rush of remorse. The kiss that hadn't been given, the hasty word later regretted, all that kind of thing.

And now the attack was coming in again.

Men were streaming up from below, making for the upper

decks fore and aft, some of them climbing to the flight deck, the furthest from the sea. Cameron used his megaphone as the ship wallowed, back now in the trough of a much decreased sea. 'Lower whalers and cutters as soon as ready. All Carley floats to be launched now. After that it's every man for himself. And the best of luck to you all.'

As he finished speaking the torpedoes hit. They took the carrier broadside to port, two of them, one for'ard, one aft. Another took the *Invergarry* amidships, breaking her into two halves that for a few moments stood upright in the water before vanishing beneath a great cloud of smoke and flame and escaping steam from her boilers.

Cameron, as the torpedoes struck, both of them in almost the same instant, was blown clear over the side.

Ben Malting struggled through the water towards Cameron, who was floating head down about a cable's-length away from the carrier, now in her death throes with steam coming up from every crack and break in her shattered sides. A strong swimmer, Malting grabbed hold of Cameron, turned him over, and towed him towards the nearest Carley float, already filling with men and others holding fast to the life-lines drooping over its side. Malting got a grip with his left hand, his right holding fast to Cameron, who he reckoned was alive still. In one of the lowered whalers sat Mr Trimby with his anxieties. An obvious corpse drifted past: Chief Petty Officer Stoner, his chest no more than a gaping hole. His old parents were due for terrible news, as he had feared since the start of the war. Another corpse was Master-at-Arms Horner, but masters-at-arms, like chief gunner's mates, had never had parents: they were quarried, not born of woman.

Captain Mason-Goodson left his ship at last, not after all by way of tilted plank but by way of an explosive force which rent him into fragments of flesh that mingled with those of the committal guard and others who had been in the vicinity of the body.

The JU 88s did not come back for a strafing attack on the

169

survivors. To that extent, they were lucky. Cameron, coming round to find himself lying flat in the bottom of the Carley float, was put in the picture of events by Ben Malting.

'She's gone, sir. So's *Invergarry*. And not all that number of survivors.' Malting paused. 'How're you feeling, sir?'

'Groggy. But don't worry about me. We'll make a count of who's still with us.' Cameron grinned, tightly. 'A sort of muster by the Open List.' Banter often helped; Malting played along with it.

'That's for pay days only, sir. Once a bleeding fortnight.'

'When's the next one?'

'Lost count, sir.'

'Too bad. But perhaps we'll be in Pompey by then.'

'Let's hope you're right, sir,' Malting said with feeling. 'How d'you rate the chances of us being picked up?'

'That's a question for higher authority. In the meantime. . . .' Cameron heaved himself into a sitting position, feeling groggy still and light-headed. He looked around at the little fleet of boats and Carley floats: he still had a command and he would exercise it to the best of his ability. 'We keep together,' he went on, 'and we keep cheerful. There should be enough hard rations and water to last a while – '

'No Bible, sir?'

'No Bible. For a start, we have a sing-song. You're used to pubs. Where they sing. You start us off. Anything you like and I don't mind how vulgar.'

Malting started off and gradually they all joined in. The adventures of Old King Cole who got up to some very odd practices in the middle of the night, all the boats and floats together. It was corny but there were not many classical music lovers amongst the ship's company and it helped a lot.

That last-minute message from the rescue tugs, target of the first attack by the JU 88s had got through, as had, later, a transmission from *Invergarry* just before the end had come. This time the reaction in the Admiralty was immediate: a destroyer escorting a homeward-bound convoy from Halifax,

Nova Scotia, was ordered to detach to the position given by *Invergarry*, proceeding at her maximum speed. Scarcely had the destroyer altered course away from the convoy when the unctuous, traitorous tones of Lord Haw-Haw came on the air from Berlin.

'This is Gairmany calling . . . the wives and families of the men aboard the British aircraft-carrier *Charger* should be asking the infamous demon Churchill about the fate of their loved ones. This morning our glorious Führer authorized an attack on a British force in the North Atlantic in the course of which successful attack the aircraft-carrier and her escort were sunk with all hands. . . .'

There would be unnecessary tears in at least some homes throughout Britain until the rescuing destroyer made contact with the boats and rafts.